VOLUME

TALES
OF
NOVIA

USA TODAY BESTSELLING AUTHOR
JESSICA CAGE

Dragonia

Preciosa

Tendrils

Skinoshi Falls

the Hve

Gilden

Scarnious

Titan's Hold

NOVIA

Kilosh
Ethos
Civilus
The Mills
Warpen Forest
Havenpoint
Sabrine
Lake
Kasial's Ruins
Mosail
Lesera
Halos
Mt Niccoli
Moon Hollow

Written by Jessica Cage

Edited by Naomi Nakashima
Cover Design by: Celin Graphics
Book Design by: Jessica Cage
Copyright © 2022 Jessica Cage

ISBN-13: **978-1-958295-11-3**

To my son who continues to inspire me each day with your amazing imagination. In the moments when all this seems so impossible, I look at you and I'm proven wrong.

By Sight and Song

JESSICA CAGE

ONE

Shanoai woke in a clichéd fashion, drenched in her own sweat. This was the twelfth night in a row that she had the dream, and each night it felt more real. She lay there, staring at the lights that moved across the ceiling. The reflection of the moonlight bouncing off the seas.

"You had the dream again, didn't you?" Charlie groaned as she shifted in the bed next to Shanoai.

"I'm sorry, I didn't mean to wake you." Shanoai looked over at her wife and glanced at the plump ass that was still pointed in her direction.

"It's fine." Charlie rolled over to face her and pushed aside the bright red hair that slipped from beneath Shanoai's bonnet. "Are you okay?"

"Yeah. Just wish I could figure out why I keep having these dreams." Shanoai sighed, turning to the window and to look out at the moon. "Nothing about them makes sense. I keep trying to decipher a purpose for it, but hell if I know what it's all supposed to mean."

"What happened this time?" Charlie yawned. "Was it the same as before?"

"Yes, it's always the same. That's the worst part, you know. I wait for something to change, but it's the same every time. I'm at some broken-down church and there is something dark there, a being I can't see. Only–"

"What?" Charlie perked up. "What happened?"

"Now that I think about it, it was different this time. Something changed." Shanoai touched her forehead as if trying to bring the dream back. "What was it? Something happened that doesn't usually happen."

"Can you remember what it was?" Charlie sat up and reached for the notepad by the desk. Since the dreams started, she kept detailed notes about them. The observations were the same each time, but this time there was a chance for something more.

"I..." Shanoai pressed her hands against her face. "Oh."

"What?" Charlie sat perched on her knees, pen tip to the page.

"I saw his face." Shanoai sat up. "The being. The figure I can never make out, this time I saw his face and then he disappeared."

"What did he look like?" She scribbled on the pad, her long braids creating a curtain around her face as she wrote.

"I don't know. Dark skin, dark eyes, there were a lot of shadows. It was almost like he commanded them." She said with a frown.

"He commanded shadows?" Charlie looked at her wife wearing a matching grimace. "I thought you said he was a vampire, or at least that's the feeling you got before." She flipped through her notes.

"He is. I saw his fangs, definitely vampire." Shanoai shook her head. "Since when can a vampire move shadows? It sounds insane, right?"

"Maybe not. Maybe it's a good thing that you finally saw something more. How do you feel?"

"I don't know." Shanoai laid back down. "It doesn't matter. It's not like it means anything."

"All dreams mean something." Charlie finished her note and returned the pad to the nightstand. "We just have to figure out what the message is."

"Not in Mosail." Shanoai huffed, her disappointment clear. "Not when you don't have the vision."

"Shan, don't do this to yourself again." Charlie pulled Shanoai's hand into hers.

"You're right. I need to stop beating myself up. Not like it's easy, you know. The broken seer." Shanoai shifted in the bed. "You know that's what they call me. They all thought I was going to be some great visionary and here I am with no power at all."

"You're not alone there, you know. The lack of power." Charlie reminded her. "Most of us don't have power. We're just normal beings."

"Yeah, well, most of us aren't like me. My mother was a powerful seer and my father... Well, we know what my father was." Shanoai sighed. "I don't mean to dismiss you, you know that. I'm sorry."

"I know you don't mean it that way. You don't have to apologize to me."

"I just, I wanted to make her proud. To make losing her life to bring me into the world worth it. Every day that I go without a vision just feels like another day I disappoint her."

"I doubt your mother would ever feel anything less than pride." Charlie caressed her wife's jaw. "You're amazing in so many ways, even if you can't see it."

The Selective, those descendants of the original seers, looked at Shanoai differently because of who her parents were. The daughter of two powerful beings, and yet she had no powers to call her own.

Her mother was a seer, her father a pixie. They made an unlikely pair, but they somehow made it work despite how many people preferred they not be together. This pairing set her bloodline up to be the strongest, but as she grew to maturity, she displayed no signs of the power they expected. Instead of being protected, they ridiculed and mocked her for her unremarkable remarkableness.

She spent most of her life just trying to prove to the rest of her people that she did, in fact, possess power, however limited it might be. But they refused to believe her because she'd already disappointed them. She failed all the tests and only ever reported

4

visions of the sea, nothing that could be verified. Eventually, even those strange occurrences stopped and she gave up on trying to connect with the gift she felt belonged to her.

As Charlie said, not everyone born to the Selective, possessed the gift of vision. Though there were others without power, Shanoai was the only one ever ridiculed for it. It was bad enough her mother married and reproduced with a pixie. The least she could have done was to be born with some special abilities, something to aid in the advancement of her people.

If she were a boy, it would have been easier. Every man was born without vision, as their goddess only gifted the power to those whose intuition matched her own—women. Of the women, only thirty percent had visions, but that rate dwindled every year.

When Shanoai couldn't aid her people through sight, she joined the guard, choosing a path that she believed would make her worthy in the eyes of the Selective. She was wrong. Even as she promised to lay her life on the line in battle, they taunted her.

After she shot to the top ranks of her class in the academy, they heckled her as she crossed the stage to receive her well-earned awards. Nothing she did could ever get her away from the way they saw her. A broken promise with broken vision.

The first time she had what she thought was a vision, she ran to the Sukra, the eldest of the seers. She reported what she saw and for two days, she felt elated. Having a vision meant she was no longer broken, and her people loved her for it. But when the scouts returned with their findings, proving her vision to be nothing more than a lucid dream, it sent her back to the corner. Only this time, her shame was public.

The reports of her false lead spread through the city of Mosail. And everywhere she went, she heard whispers and saw fingers pointed in her direction. Things were only just settling down and there she was again, having dreams that felt like something more.

"Maybe you could take it to the Sukra again." Charlie offered. "Maybe they'll be able to figure this out."

"Yeah right. You want me to sign up to be the joke of the city again?" Shanoai scoffed at the idea of taking details of her dreams to the seer elders. The women had already laughed her out of their temple once. The entire city knew of her attempt to bring her vision to light. She refused to go through that embarrassment again.

"This feels different though," Charlie rubbed her shoulder. "You said it yourself. This is more than a dream. It means something."

"It might, hell, it feels like it does." Shanoai looked at her and smiled when those bright green eyes looked back at her. "I love you, but there is no way in hell am I going back there."

"Well, it's your decision." Charlie leaned over to kiss Shanoai and smiled. "Try to get some sleep. We have a big day ahead of us tomorrow. New recruits to train."

"Of course, must be ready to kick some newbie tail." Shanoai turned to her side, scooping Charlie into a spoon. She tried to sleep, but each time she drifted off, the dark stranger visited her again.

"It happened again, didn't it?" Charlie yawned as she sat up in bed.

"What do you mean?" Shanoai entered the bedroom with a fresh cup of califer in her hand.

They brewed the tea from an orange flower with golden webbed veining. Ingesting the plant kept the Seer people closer to the light of their ancestors. The steam lifted from the warm drink, bringing the aroma of lavender with it. She always put lavender leaves in her morning brew, especially after a night of fitful dreams.

"Don't play coy. You had the dream again. I could feel you stirring all night. It must have been intense." After a deep yawn, she inhaled the scent of the tea. "Lavender, we both know what that means, Shan."

"Yes, I do." She blew on her cup, cooling the contents before taking a quick sip. "But I'm okay."

"You keep saying that, but it's getting worse." Charlie confronted her. "The dreams are more intense and our lavender supply is lower than ever."

"I'm fine." Shanoai handed her a cup of the aromatic tea and kissed her on the forehead.

"I'm worried. This isn't normal."

"We've already confirmed that nothing about me is normal, Charlie. Why should this be any different?"

"You may be right, but that doesn't mean I won't worry about you." Charlie blew on the tea to cool it before she took a sip.

"This is why I love you, woman." Shanoai was about to kiss

Charlie again, but there was a knock on the door.

"Who could be here this early?" Charlie looked past her wife towards the front door of their small house. "The sun is barely up."

"I don't know, but whoever it is, I'll get rid of them."

Shanoai left Charlie alone in the bedroom and headed for the front door. Their house was small, but it was perfect for them, right by the water and away from the general population. The house belonged to her mother, and when Shanoai came of age, she took it over. If someone was knocking on their door, it had to be something serious.

The knocking sounded again. Whoever was there to visit wasn't patient.

"I'm coming, cool it!" Shanoai called out as she tripped over the rug and cursed under her breath. "What?" She swung the door open, then froze. "Oh."

"Shanoai Angelus." The Cisk said her name. Cisk was the golden-robed guards, the highest level a guard could reach, and the personal protectors of the Sukra. And they were knocking on her door.

"That's me, but you already know that." All of Mosail knew who Shanoai was, especially the Cisk.

"Your presence has been requested." They said with a straight face.

"The Sukra wants to see me? Why?" She asked. What could

the elder seers possibly want with her?

"That information wasn't divulged to us. We were told to retrieve you. Please gather your things."

"What's going on?" Charlie exited the bedroom and looked around Shanoai to the guards at the door. "What are they doing here?"

"Apparently the Sukra have summoned me." Shanoai looked over her shoulder at her wife, who pulled a robe around her body when she saw their guests.

"What? Do you think–" She started.

"I think we should get dressed and go find out what they want." Shanoai cut her off. If they didn't already know about her dreams, she wouldn't be offering the information.

"Right, okay. I'll go get dressed." Charlie left Shanoai alone with the Cisk.

"We will wait outside." The guard said.

"Sure thing."

Shanoai winked and closed the door in their face.

"Do you believe this shit?" She cursed as she returned to the bedroom.

"What?" Charlie asked, peaking her head out of the closet.

"What gives them the right to summon me? Sending the Cisk to come and retrieve me like I'm some kind of object."

"Shan, what's the problem?" Charlie asked. "You're a guardian, just like I am. It's not unheard of for the Sukra to request guardians to come to council."

"Right. But when was the last time any of them volunteered to see me? When was the last time they asked to have me come there? I've been the top of my class, first in my rank for a decade now, and not once did they call me. Now... now that I'm having this fucked up dream they want to chat. That's no coincidence."

"You think it's because of the dream?" Charlie pulled a top over her head and struggled with her braids.

"Yes, unless you have some other theory." Shanoai's gut told her she was right. The Sukra knew about her dreams even without her reporting them.

Charlie chewed her bottom lip. "I don't."

"Yeah. Neither do I."

"Well, we can sit around here speculating or we can see what they have to say." Charlie pointed to the front door. "I gotta tell you, I don't think they're going to allow us to just go on about our day as scheduled."

"Fuck. I don't want to deal with this shit." Shanoai retrieved her tea and took a long sip.

"Well, let's get it over with. Hey, maybe it's something simple.

Maybe they just want to wish you a happy belated birthday."

"Right because they're so concerned about me turning a year older."

"Hey, how many times are you going to turn thirty-five? It's a big deal."

"To you." Shanoai smirked. "I would much rather forget it happened."

"It's okay, you know I like your old ass." Charlie crossed the room, pulled Shanoai into her arms, and kissed her.

"Damn right you do." Shanoai smiled, then groaned with the Cisk pounded on the door. "We're coming dammit!"

"We could make them wait a little longer." Charlie flashed a devilish grin.

"Hell, what's the worst they can do?" Shanoai lifted Charlie and carried her to the bed.

TWO

The Cisks weren't happy about how long they were made to wait, which put a big smile on Shanoai's face. A smile that faded as they neared the inner circle of Mosail. The home of the seers comprised a series of interconnecting circles that spiraled inward until they reached the very center where Aloi, their temple, stood. This was the place where the Sukra met and where the visions of the seers were put to the test.

They traveled through the city on controlled currents of air. Those of the Selective that didn't have vision were often born with other talents. Those gifts were tied to the elements. Most often connecting to either air or water. It was the magic of the Alairians, those with the affinity for air that controlled the currents and passageways for the guardians. Again, another reason Shanoai was a disappointment. Not only did she not have vision, but she also had no affinity, nothing to be used to support her people.

They stepped from the current right in front of Aloi and the Cisks headed straight up the stairs to the temple. Shanoai and Charlie followed but let some distance fall between them.

"Are you okay here?" Charlie asked.

"Yeah, I mean, how bad can it be? They just want to talk, so let's just hear them out. As far as I know, I've done nothing to be punished for."

"You're the picture of perfection, the model citizen." Charlie poked her in the side.

"Let's hope they see it that way." Shanoai laughed as they entered the doors.

Her laughter came to a sharp end as they saw the large flame above the jade pillar. A flame that was only lit when the Sukra witnessed a grand vision, something they thought would effectually change the course for the Selective.

"That can't be good." Shanoai mumbled, and Charlie grabbed her hand.

"You got this." Charlie whispered. "I'm right here."

They passed the pillar and to the massive double doors that stood behind it. The entrance to Sai, the inner temple to the room only used by the Sukra. When a seer had a vision that could affect the world as a whole, the Sukra were called to consort. Shanoai expected someone to come out to deliver a message. Instead, the doors opened and the Cisk ushered them inside.

Hands still joined, the couple walked through the doors and came face to face with the members of the Sukra.

"Shanoai, I'm glad you're here." Waoli, the eldest of the Sukra, addressed her as she entered the temple of Sai. She sat at the center of the crescent table, dressed in white robes that matched the flow of coarse hair that fell past her shoulders. Her skin was the smooth tone of desert sands, and her eyes were bright orbs of sunlight. When she looked at a person, she made them feel safe and warm.

Eight other elders sat at the table, four on either side of her, all dressed in robes of various colors. Each woman was of a different imposition. Some weighed on the mind, others on the heart, but they all invaded anyone who laid eyes on them. It was what happened when a seer became a Sukra. Their gifted immortality amplified their powers. Not all seers were immortal, but the Sukra were.

"You are?" Shanoai smirked. "That's a first. Usually, people are ready for me to leave before I even get in the room."

"Yes, well, this time is different." Mauor, another of the Sukra, commented.

She was a rigid seer. Her burnt orange robes blended with the orange undertones of her brown skin. Her eyes were dark gray and full of pessimism.

"How is it different?" Shanoai asked, nervous about their response.

"You've had visions, haven't you?" Waoli asked with a gentle voice and a small smile.

"And you would believe me if I said yes now? Why?" Shanoai felt like she was losing her mind. Why did they suddenly believe her? What changed?

"We've had confirmation," Waoli answered. "News from the

Peacekeepers of a great disturbance in the Tendrils."

"Are you serious?" Shanoai blanched as flashes of her dream passed through her mind. The run-down building where the mutated vampire lived. It was in the Tendrils.

"We do not call people into our temple if we are not serious about our remarks." Mauor spoke again with a disapproving frown.

"You'll have to excuse me. My entire life, you've all fed me the idea that I was broken. You told me my vision was nothing more than a lucid dream and now you're telling me that all this time I was right and you were wrong. And you only believe it now because a Peacekeeper told you."

"Shanoai," Charlie shot her a warning glance.

"No, that is alright. Her skepticism is valid." Waoli held her hand up. "You know we do not move on visions without tangible proof they will come to pass. The things we see can always change."

"So, what do you want from me now?" Shanoai asked, her anger still brewing.

Yes, it felt good to for once have someone validate her concerns, but it was a slap in the face that they hadn't been on her side the entire time.

"We want you to help us deal with this. It is what we trained you to do." Mauor chimed in. "Or are you refusing your post now?"

"I would never turn my back on my people." Shanoai's chest puffed up as she spoke. She took pride in her position as a guardian. It was the one thing she'd never failed at.

"What is happening in the Tendrils must be taken care of. The peacekeeper says that they have contained it, but he doesn't believe that it will not turn into something worse." Again, Waoli followed her with a softer comment. "This is a lot to ask of you. I understand your position. We all do. It is okay if you choose not to help with this, but we think you are the best person for the job."

Shanoai looked around the candlelit room and considered her options. She could walk away with her head high, knowing she was right, and let them figure it out without her. But her gut told her that was the wrong thing to do. Her visions came for a reason. The goddess chose her to see the way. She wouldn't disregard that, no matter how much she wanted to stick it to the Sukra for rejecting her for so long.

"How could I possibly be of service here?" Shanoai asked and saw Charlie smile out of the corner of her eye. Charlie's happiness, her approval, was all that Shanoai needed.

"We need you to speak with Saxfy, the Pixie Queen." Mauor offered. "The peacekeeper says she has something that can help. You'll need to leave immediately."

"The queen?" Shanoai almost choked on her words. "Wait, you mean you want me to go because I'm half pixie. Again, after years of being mocked for it, you now want to use it to your advantage."

Charlie tightened her hold on Shanoai's hand, giving her a

reminder to keep her calm. The Sukra would only take so much from her and she was already on thin ice with her outburst. Shanoai took a deep breath before continuing to address them.

"You want me to go there and do what? Say that I have pixie blood in my veins, so they owe me a meeting with their queen? You know how they are. They would cut my head off before I even get past the gates."

"If this goes unchecked–" Mauor started.

"Yeah, I know, grave danger for all." Shanoai finished the thought. If not, the Sukra wouldn't have bothered to bring her in. They'd have the Cisks handle it and never look back.

"Will you help us or should we look elsewhere?" Mauor asked.

Shanoai huffed. "Of course, I will. I'm not petty enough to turn my back on my people now."

"Wait," Charlie spoke.

"What is it?" Mauor asked, annoyed that she had the nerve to address them. This meeting was about Shanoai, not her wife.

"You need to make this right." Charlie spoke to Waoli, the more sensible member of the Sukra. "All this time you've been saying that Shanoai doesn't have vision, but she does. It might not work the way we think it should, but it's there. She deserves the same respect and the same ceremony as any other born with the gift."

18

"Charlie," Shanoai grabbed her wife's wrist. "It's fine."

"You want us to perform the Kino for her?" Mauor guffawed.

"Yes, she may not be petty enough to turn her back on you, but I am." Charlie looked at her wife, then back to the Sukra. "For years, our people have pushed her to the side, dismissed her even though she lays her life on the line for us. And now that you need her, you expect it to be without making amends for that?"

"Careful," Muaor warned.

"Or what? You would punish me for pointing out your flaws?" Charlie asked. "What does that tell the rest of our people? Never question the Sukra, never tell them they are wrong, because even if they are, they won't admit it. They won't make things right."

The Sukra erupted in a clamor as they discussed hosting a Kino, the rising ceremony for Shanoai. During the Kino, they presented the new seer to the goddess beneath the moonlight. It was a time to thank her for their blessing and most came out of it with a deeper connection to their powers.

Most were against the public display, but there were a few who agreed with what Charlie said. Shanoai had the gift of vision. What she saw was true. The goddess gave her a gift, even if they didn't understand how that gift worked. And for that, she deserved the same respect that the others gifted with sight received.

Waoli held up her hand, ending the conversation of the others. When they quieted, she spoke.

"Charlie is right. Shanoai has vision and should be treated as

such. There is no reason we shouldn't afford her the same care."
The elder Sukra announced. "I will not put this up for debate. We
need her strong for this journey and communing with our goddess
can only lend to her strength. We will not refuse this wish."

"We will prepare for the ceremony." Mauor spoke with
resignation.

"Are there any other demands?" Waoli asked with a small
smile.

"No, that is all." Charlie nodded, and Shanoai shrugged.

"Great. Then you two might want to go prepare for your trip.
You have a long way to go." Waoli instructed and a moment later
the Cisks returned to the room and ushered the couple out of the
temple. As they left, Waoli gave orders for the preparations for
Shanoai's ceremony.

"That wasn't necessary." Shanoai whispered to Charlie as
they descended the steps to the street.

"Like hell! You deserve this. Everyone said you were wrong,
they denied your vision." Charlie calmed, then continued with
an apologetic tone. "Even me. We all owe you an apology. That
ceremony is your birthright. Don't let them take that away from
you."

"Charlie, I don't need all of this." Shanoai shook her head.
"Hell, part of me doesn't want anyone to know."

"Why would you not want anyone to know?" Charlie asked,
confused.

"Because they'll expect something of me. Again. What if this was a solo event? What if it's a coincidence and it never happens again?"

"What if it's not? And so what? There are seers who only ever have a handful of visions their entire life. It doesn't make their gift any less impressive. They still get respect in our community. You deserve it too, Shan."

"You won't let this go, will you?" Shanoai asked. She knew the look on Charlie's face. She was determined to get her way in this.

"No, I won't." Charlie kissed her, then frowned. "Shanoai, I'm sorry."

"For what?" She looked down at her wife.

"I doubted you and I shouldn't have. I should have been more supportive." She admitted. "I just wanted them to treat you better, and I wanted you to feel you belong here. I know that you never have."

"You've been plenty supportive, and I understand why you and everyone else doubted me. I've only gotten visions of one thing, and that's not the way it typically works." Shanoai looked back at the temple. "At least now I don't have to feel like I'm crazy."

"Is that how you feel? Crazy?" Charlie looked like her heart broke to hear Shanoai's truth.

"Well, yeah. I mean, I failed all the tests. Had no inkling of connection to the goddess. When this started, and they rejected my report, I did everything in my power to convince myself that they were just very vivid dreams. I'm just happy to be heard now and believed. Maybe I can disconnect from these visions now."

"Is that what you want, for your visions to end?" Charlie frowned. "After all this time, you don't want it?"

"Not end, maybe just change?" Shanoai put her arm around Charlie's shoulder. "It would be nice to have control like some others do. Or to not have them come as nightmares."

"Maybe the ceremony will help that happen." Charlie nodded. "I, for one, will be glad to get more sleep."

"Oh, you don't love me waking you up every night in a cold sweat?" Shanoai laughed. "I guess we should prepare for that, huh?"

THREE

When they returned to Aloi, it was transformed. Even though Mauor was against the ceremony, she refused to have her reputation tarnished by half-assing the occasion. Typically, they had a few weeks to prepare for the Kino, but they had less than a day. The sun was setting and the moon rising, which meant little time for them to work. Shanoai had to be ready when the moon was at its highest point in the sky.

As soon as they arrived, the Cisks swept her away from Charlie and escorted her to the room for preparations. The temple was busy with people completing details. The caliper flower hung everywhere, along with yellow crystals meant to capture the light of the moon. As the moon rose, they absorbed more power from it. Power that would be used in the ceremony.

They removed her clothes. She'd come in her guardian gear, ready for battle, not for communing with the goddess. They traded her boots for sandals and her pants and coat for soft flowing robes made of a unique fabric called hazen lace. The lace makers created the material using a special process that blended air and water into the threading. The material floated without air, which made it perfect for the ceremony.

When Shanoai entered the temple, led by aides, she quickly found Charlie's face. Standing at the front of the ceremony room by the moon pool. It was when she saw her wife's face that she relaxed. She did this for Charlie, because Shanoai would have gladly left without the ceremony being performed.

Waoli stood at the center in robes matching Shanoai's.

"We welcome Shanoai Angelus, daughter of Lorilei Angelus, to the moon pool where she will commune with our goddess and show thanks for the gift given to her."

Usually full of cheer, the room was silent as she walked down the aisle to meet Waoli.

"Are you ready?" The elder asked.

"Yes." Shanoai nodded.

"Very well, let's begin." Waoli swept her hand toward the pool and a cool flow of air moved to the room.

Shanoai nodded and as she moved forward, the aides pulled the robe from her shoulders, leaving her in a sheer dress made of the same fabric. She looked at Charlie, who gave her a reassuring nod before she continued.

She walked into the pool, slowly taking the steps down as her body adjusted to the cool water. The dress, designed like the petals of the caliper flower, flowed out around her in a halo as she moved.

She turned around to see Waoli enter the pool, and as the elder seer stepped in, the water took on a new chill that crawled up her spine and arrested her heart. She stared at the woman and when their eyes met, the warmth of her golden iris reached within Shanoai, releasing her from the frost.

Waoli walked to the middle of the water to meet Shanoai, grabbed her hands, and smiled before turning back to the rest of the crowd.

"This is a moment to be celebrated. Our goddess blesses few with the gift of vision. We rejoice when this moment comes. As the moon reaches its peak in the sky, we are closest to She who breathes life into us. Let us bathe in her light and pay thanks for the gift of vision that Sister Shanoai receives."

The elder spread her arms out and held her palms open to the temple. The cool show of air, her affinity, moved around them and the crystals that were positioned around the room, all imbued with the power of the rising moon, lit up light stars on Earth. Slowly, they lifted from their bases, and as they rose, their light grew brighter.

Then the light pulled from each crystal and shot into the water, replacing the chill with warmth. Shanoai watched in awe and tried to appreciate every detail of an experience she'd only witnessed before.

Waoli turned to Shanoai as the light continued to fill the pool. "This is your moment, Shanoai. The goddess awaits you. Welcome her with an open heart and allow her love to flow in."

Shanoai nodded, and Waoli turned and left the pool. Standing at the pool's edge, the elder welcomed the other Sukra to join her. They did, all nine lined up at the edge of the pool and knelt beside it. Waoli was the last. One by one, they touched their fingertips to the center of their forehead, lips, and heart, then dipped their hands in the water.

The water hummed with the power of the seers, each one lending to feeling. Shanoai remained still. As the water charged more, she felt it moving her, slowly lifting her body until she was out of the water. Her body then shifted to be parallel to the surface of the water.

Beneath her, the water moved in spirals, creating the image of an eye that opened up to the moon above her. Shanoai looked down to see the amazing movement of the water before she looked at the sky.

"Open your heart, feel Her love." Waoli's voice came in a low hum to Shanoai.

She closed her eyes and tried to push all reservations from her mind. She thought of love, of the things that brought her happiness, of Charlie, and the smile spread across her face.

At that moment, vapors rose from the water in thin wisps that danced around her body. As they moved, they became so dense that she could no longer see the other people in the temple.

Consumed by the fog, Shanoai could see only one thing, the moon above her. The ceiling above the moon pool had retracted, leaving the room open to the night sky and as the moon reached its highest point. When it finally reached its peak, the light filled the room, shooting down in a powerful beam that she opened her arms to accept.

The light washed out everything else and Shanoai felt tingles run across her body and the soft whispers of a voice she couldn't make out. It was female, nurturing, and made her feel complete for the first time in her life. She wanted to hold on to the feeling, to live in that moment forever, but it would not last.

Shock replaced comfort, and she seized. A surge of power flowed through her accompanies by the light from the moon stopped, and she fell into the pool below. It wasn't the gentle return everyone had. The impact sent a splash of water into the faces of the Sukra.

When the fog cleared, Shanoai stood from the water, and everyone gasped. Her eyes, usually a cool mix of honey and gray, were lit bright white, the light of the moon filtering through her. She opened her mouth to speak, but no words came out.

"Shan?" Charlie's voice was a whisper, but it was enough to grab her attention.

She looked at her, softened, then fell again into the water.

"Shan!" Charlie ran into the pool and pulled Shanoai from the water. "What the hell was that?" She looked up at the elder as she cradled her wife in her arms.

"I don't know. This has never happened before." Waoli stood and gestured to her aides, who entered the water and pulled Shanoai from Charlie's arms.

"What are you doing? Where are you taking her?" She asked, panicked.

"We need to take her to heal. We need her whole." Waoli

spoke. "You can come with her."

Charlie nodded, climbed from the water, and followed the aides, who carried Shanoai's limp body past the terrified faces of the attending members of the Selective.

FOUR

"**C**harlie?" Shanoai groaned, her eyes opening for the first time since she fell into the pool.

"Shan?" Charlie sat by the bedside where she'd been since the healers finished their work. There was nothing physically wrong with Shanoai, so all they could do was wait for her to wake up.

"What's going on? Where am I?" Shanoai lifted her head to look around the plain room.

"The infirmary." Charlie answered.

"What? Why?" Shanoai panicked and tried to get out of the bed. "What happened to me?"

"You're okay," Charlie reassured her while pushing her back down.

"If I'm okay, why am I here?" Shanoai looked her wife in the eye. "They don't put people who are perfectly fine in the infirmary, Charlie."

"Do you remember anything?" She touched her forehead, still ignoring Shanoai's question.

"Is there something I should remember? Just tell me what happened." Shanoai became irritated. She didn't like being in the dark about whatever happened to her.

"You passed out after the ceremony." Charlie took a deep breath as she gathered her thoughts. "I ran into the water to get you, to stop you from drowning."

"What?" Shanoai shook her head. "I do not remember that. The last thing I remember is light, powerful warm light washing over me, and then nothing."

"I'm just glad you're okay." Charlie relaxed, worry no longer wrinkling the corners of her eyes.

"She's awake, good." The Cisk stepped into the room. "How do you feel?"

"I'm okay." Shanoai sat up.

"Good, because Waoli wants to see you." They reported, right to business.

"She just woke up." Charlie snapped. "Give her time."

"Time is not on our side and we already lost a full day on her little nap." The Cisk didn't care about Shanoai needing time to recover. They had orders and that was all that mattered.

"A day?" Shanoai asked. "I've been sleeping for a day?"

"Yes." Charlie turned. "Give her time. They denied her vision for this long. It's on their heads if time isn't on our side now."

"Fine." The Cisk turned to leave. "I'll be sure to let Waoli know how you feel."

"You do that." She snapped. "Can you believe them? Like it's going to kill them to give you time to rest. You aren't going out there to put your neck on the line for them if they're going to treat you like this."

"Are you going to keep going to war for me?" Her lips lifted in a small smile as Shanoai looked at her wife. If there was one thing she could count on, it was Charlie making sure no one ever took advantage of her.

"As long as I need to." Charlie touched her wife's head. The same red hair slipped from the bonnet she made sure they put on her head. Shanoai took great care of her hair and it would have upset her to wake and find it matted to her head with sweat.

"My little spitfire." Shanoai smiled. "But I am okay to meet with Waoli. As she said, something big is coming. And as much as I would love to lie here and rest up, I can't stay here knowing that whatever that thing is may be out there hurting people."

"Are you sure?" Charlie asked. "I know you, Shan. You put everyone above yourself. Don't do that right now."

"Yes." Shanoai grabbed Charlie's hand on brought it to her lips. "I promise, I'm okay to go."

"Fine, I'll get the Cisk back in here." Charlie got up to leave.

"Charlie!" Shanoai called to her.

"Yes, Shan?" She turned back to her, a hint of worry in her expression.

"I love you. You know that?"

"Of course, I do." She winked at her and left the room.

It wasn't long until she returned with the Cisk, who impatiently waited for them to gather Shanoai's things.

"Where are we going?" Shanoai asked as the Cisk led them from the infirmary in the opposite direction of the Aloi, where they assumed they would meet Waoli. "Why aren't we going back to the temple?"

"This meeting is not with the Sukra, it is with Waoli." The Cisk looked back over his shoulder.

"Okay." Shanoai caught Charlie's eye in a glance, and they both frowned.

They continued through a passage that dropped beneath the ground. The dark passage was dark. The only light from crystals charged with the light of the moon. They flickered softly like stars beneath the earth. They were underground for ten minutes before the path inclined back to the surface. When they exited the hidden passage, they were in the middle of a large room. Warm air circled through the space, creating a calm that relaxed them.

"Shanoai, welcome." Waoli's voice echoed around them before she appeared. "And you as well, Charlie." She smiled.

"Thank you for inviting us into your home." Shanoai responded softly. "But why are we meeting here? Why not Aloi?"

"I have my reasons." Waoli looked at the Cisk, who reentered the path beneath the floor, leaving them alone to talk in private. "Are you hungry? I have fish, veggies, and oh, the most delicious treat from earth! Raw Oysters. Don't ask me how, but I've fallen in love with the things."

"No, I'm okay." Shanoai frowned at the platter. The thought of food made her nauseous, but she wouldn't tell either of them that.

"You don't want people to know we are meeting." Charlie said, also refusing the offered meal.

"Very astute." Waoli smiled before devouring an oyster. "There are people who I no longer trust, people who, if they knew we were speaking right now, wouldn't like it. Things are shifting. There is a darkness is rolling in and I fear that this darkness has already corrupted some of our own."

"What people?" Shanoai asked.

"That is not of importance now. You have a journey ahead of you, one that will be difficult enough without a list like that in your mind." The elder answered. "Weeding out the dark ones is not a responsibility I leave only to you. It is going to take a team effort. You have a part to play in it. Are you ready for that?"

"Yes." Shanoai nodded. What else was she going to say? Though the phrase, 'Hell no', sounded fitting.

"I wanted to gift you with something that might help you on your travels." Waoli opened her hand, and sitting in her palm was a small silver box with an eye etched in black on the surface.

"What is it?" Shanoai examined the box. Just as she attempted to open it, Waoli placed her hand on top of hers.

"Not now." She smiled. "It will help you when you need it. Only open it then. You'll know when it's time."

"So, a mystery box. Thanks." She shook the box next to her ear but heard nothing move inside. "Anything else? What now?"

"Now you leave," the floor opened again, and the Cisk returned.

"Okay, short and sweet." Shanoai turned, and her wife followed.

"Not you." Waoli spoke, placing her hand on Charlie's shoulder. "Shanoai's journey is not yours."

"What?" Shanoai turned back to the seer.

"Charlie, I need you to stay." Waoli spoke to her wife. "You also have a part to play in this. Your role is to stay here in Mosail."

"I–" Charlie started.

"Why?" Shanoai asked. She intended to have Charlie by her side, the way they'd been for over two decades. She was more than her love. She was her best friend.

"Again, that is not for you to be concerned about. You have a goal. Get to Preciosa, speak to the queen. You will know where to go from there." Waoli repeated Shanoai's task.

"And I'm supposed to just leave her here with you?" Shanoai glance between the elder and her wife. "Why should I trust you not to hurt her?"

"Charlie will be protected." Waoli smirked. "Not that she needs it. I have no desire to harm her."

"Shan, I'll be fine. We have to do this." Charlie nodded. "I wish I could be there with you. But if this is how it needs to be, I say we do it. I'll be with you in spirit."

"Are you sure?" Shanoai asked.

"No." She smirked. "But I believe in you. I will do whatever I have to do here to support you. Just stay safe and get your ass back here in one piece."

"I will. I promise." Shanoai pulled Charlie into her arms, hugged and kissed her.

With some hesitation, she left Charlie behind and followed the Cisk out of Waoli's house. They walked in silence through the underground tunnel back into the city streets where the Cisk left her alone by the current that would carry her home.

"You're not coming with me?" Shanoai asked. "I thought you were my escort for this adventure."

"No." The Cisk answered simply, turned and walked away.

"Such a conversationalist!" Shanoai called out at the Cisks

back, then stepped into the current.

Though the trip was short, Shanoai kept her head down and tried to call as little attention to herself as possible. She was used to being an outcast, but this felt different. Waoli's warning wasn't something that went over her head. There were people in Mosail who were not to be trusted.

A darkness was coming. That was what she said, and that darkness had apparently already touched some of their people. Seers were people of light, both from the sun and the moon. Darkness had no place in their home.

As soon as she stepped out of the current, Shanoai was on guard. She avoided entering the house until she had inspected the perimeter to make sure that no one had followed her or set a trap.

She found no tracks around the house and no tampering with the locks or windows. Maybe she was being paranoid, but when the leader of the Selective tells you to watch your back, you don't take it lightly.

Once inside, she quickly packed her things. There was an emergency bag ready for a trip already that she added a few choice weapons to. A guard always had to be ready to move out at a moment's notice.

As she headed out of the door, she stopped and turned back to the bedroom, where a small picture frame sat on the nightstand. It was a picture of Charlie. She removed it from the frame and put it in the inside pocket of her jacket.

Satisfied with her gear, weapons, and wearing her favorite

pair of combat boots, Shanoai headed out of the house. A seer with limited magic and no magical affinity. The trek to Preciosa would be a long one.

"Well, thank you, Waoli." Shanoai clapped when she found the gift on her doorstep.

An aerohorse. An animal not unlike the typical horse, it was the host of a fallen seer's magic. When a seer dies, the Wadens, those who prepared their dead for the afterlife, performed a transference. It moved the powers of the dead into other living creatures. Those creatures couldn't be another person born of the Selective. It would have been a disrespect to the goddess to give someone power after she saw them unfit.

Transferring an air affinity to a horse was the closest thing you could do to giving it wings. Instead of galloping across the land, it glided using air currents. It was quick and silent, which made it the chosen mode of transportation for the Sukra and their Cisks.

As Shanoai climbed atop the horse when the sun started rising in the sky.

"Liz," she read the name engraved on the saddle. "Pretty name for a horse. Well, Liz, you take care of me and I'll take care of you. We got a deal?"

The aerohorse neighed softly and Shanoai took that as an agreement.

"Alright, girl. Let's hit it."

FIVE

The quickest way to go would have been to run along the shore, past Celest Lake, but it was also the most dangerous due to the water dragons that lived within. Shanoai preferred not to lose her life to a sea creature who liked to pick victims from the shore. They cut through the Lesera Forest and followed the path along the borderline between Moon Hollow where the witches lived and The Den, home of the wolves.

They took off with the sun at their back, leaving Mosail behind. As Liz ran, she became one with the wind. The world moved in a blur, cutting their travel time in half. Despite how fast the animal moved, Shanoai thought it best to stop and camp for the night.

They were too close to the wolves when the sun left the sky. It would be too risky to keep going. If caught by an agitated wolf, or worse, a wolf in heat, things could get ugly for the traveler. Instead, she found a place where they could camp. It wasn't particularly active night for the wolves but still; she had to be safe, careful. Just like she promised Charlie she would.

As she settled, having secured a place to sleep for the night, Shanoai froze. Something moved in the bushes nearby. Slowly, she reached for the dagger tucked in the holster at her ankle. Weapon secure in her hand, she stood up, scanning the area, hoping to find a small animal, something she could scare off.

The noise stopped, and she waited for it to come again, but she heard nothing else. Cautiously, she tucked the blade back in its holder and went back to adjusting her area.

"Who are you?" The low voice of a woman called out from the bushes.

Shanoai cursed under her breath, knowing immediately that it was no gentle woodland creature that watched her. She thought she would be safe where she was, but obviously, she was wrong.

"I'm not here to cause any trouble," Shanoai called out. "I'm just camping for the night. As soon as the sun is up, I'll be on my way."

"Just like the others?" The voice called.

"What others?" She shook her head. "I don't know whoever you're talking about. I'm here alone, well besides Liz, my horse."

"There were two men not too long ago. They came here did the same thing that you're doing now. Set up camp for the night then moved on." The voice said, still hidden by the shadows. "You know, we don't get that many visitors around here, so you'll understand why I find it suspicious that we got three in the same week. Do you think that's something we should be concerned about? Should I report it to the pack members?"

"Look, you don't need to report anything. If it was up to me, I would have kept riding, but I didn't want to disrespect your home. I know that this is your time to roam, so I figured I would settle down, wait out the night, and get moving in the morning." Shanoai explained her reasoning and hoped that the mysterious person wouldn't turn on her.

"You're a seer, aren't you?" The voice called out again. "I can smell it on you, like hanging by the lake on a warm summer day. That's how you all smell, but with you it's different."

"Yeah, something like that." Shanoai nodded. "This would be a lot easier if I could see you."

"What's different about you?" The voice asked, ignoring her comment. "Why do you smell so different?"

"You're right. I'm not the average seer. I've been different my whole life and asking that same question. Why me? Why am I different?" Shanoai stopped. "Please come out of the shadows. I feel like a moron standing here confessing my deepest secrets to the darkness.

"Can I trust you?" The voice asked.

"No more than I can trust you right now." The seer responded honestly. If she needed to, she would do whatever it took to defend herself and survive the encounter.

There was a long pause and then the movement in the bush again. Shortly after, a woman stepped from the cover of the foliage and waved at Shanoai. She was full figured but fit and sported a short haircut.

"There, you can see me now." She waved. "You feel better?"

"Yes, actually." Shanoai examined the wolf and felt something powerful about the woman, but she couldn't figure out what it was. All she knew was that it was something potent, something important, and the curious side of her brain urged her to figure out the mystery.

This wasn't the time for investigation. Her concern was surviving the night and making sure she completed the task she set out on. She didn't know how, but she knew that the state of her people depended on it. Waoli made sure to keep her in the dark on the details. Shanoai still questioned if that was the right thing to do.

"Where are you going?" The wolf asked.

"Preciosa." Shanoai was honest. There was no reason to lie.

"You are going to visit the pixies?" She laughed. "Why the hell would you want to do that?"

"It's not exactly something I want to do. I wish I had a choice. If I had, I wouldn't be here at all. I'm a guardian, and when the boss says you go, you go." She told the half-truth, not sure if she could trust this unknown woman yet. Her gut told her she could, but she didn't even know the she-wolf's name or why she felt such a great amount of power radiating from her.

Shanoai had encountered werewolves before. And the only time she ever felt that type of power emanating from one of them was when it was an alpha. And as far as she knew, there were no female alphas of The Den. So until she figured out why this woman made her feel the way she did, she wouldn't be rushing to spill her guts.

44

"Yeah, I get that. It would be nice, you know, to move around and do what I want with no one telling me to. But when you're part of a pack, you're one with the family. It's hard to turn your back on that, or to say no, even when you know what they're doing is wrong."

"Sounds like I'm not the only one with the problem here." Shanoai tilted her head. "Trouble in wolf land?"

"Hell, everyone in the world has their problems, right?" She crossed her arms. "Wolves are no different."

"True, and with the way things have been lately, I'm surprised the world isn't already on fire."

"Tell me something. You're a seer, right? Do you see something coming? Everyone's talking about it. There is a change happening in Novia. Power is moving differently, and the energy of our world is shifting. You can feel it in the ground, in the air. Even the water tastes different lately." She ranted. "Has anyone on your side seen anything?"

"Well, as I'm sure you know, not all of us can see the future. And not all who do can rarely make anything of the visions they get. Only a select few are capable of clear vision."

"I take it you're not one of the ones who are capable of doing that?" The she-wolf asked.

"No, I'm not. But I'm going to assume that since they're sending me on this little journey, that yeah, someone saw something. Whatever they have in Preciosa, whatever message I'm supposed to receive from their queen, damn sure has something to do with it." Shanoai divulged more of her plan than she intended. "It's not every day they send a guard to talk to the head of any city, let alone a city as volatile as the one filled with paranoid pixies."

"Yeah, but you're different, right? They'll accept you." She took a good, long sniff of the air, and shook her finger in front of her face. "That's what it is. That's what's different about you. It's hard to tell at first, but if you hang around long enough, and you know, really get a feel for the flavor, you can catch it. You're not just a seer, are you? You're part pixie."

"I could say no, but we both know I'd be lying and right now I don't think I want to lie to a werewolf on her own territory." Shanoai nodded. "Yes, I am half pixie."

"Well then, what the hell is a hybrid of a pixie and a seer doing as a guardian?" The woman stood beneath the moon and the light touched her deep brown skin and brought a soft glow that made her look almost ethereal. "Shouldn't you be like one of the most powerful things walking?"

"That's what everyone thought, but apparently I live to disappoint." Shanoai stopped herself from staring at the wolf. She didn't want her to take her appreciation for something more sinister. "I don't have powers. I only have a partial vision that's only worked once in my life and it wasn't a clear vision.

"It was all murky and full of hidden meaning. So this is the way I aid my people. This is the way I carry my weight, by being a guardian, protecting the Selective. That's not why I'm here. I have no problem with the wolves."

"Good." The woman dropped her hands to her side. "I believe you. Besides, I would have smelled it by now if you were a liar."

"Why are you out here?" Shanoai asked her own questions. "Something tells me you're not just trying to patrol the area."

"You're right, I'm not on a patrol. Actually, this is one area we hardly check. Too close to the Hue, most people avoid it. Which makes it a great place for a girl who wants to get away." She sighed. "I had a lot of my mind and went for a walk. This has been my private area for so long. I come here when I need to clear my head. But it seems with all the changes in the world, another one is that people aren't that scared of the portal that rips you away from this one."

"What's on your mind? Maybe discussing it with a passing stranger will help." Shanoai offered to be her sounding board.

"Wouldn't that be nice?" The wolf replied.

"Look. I spilled my guts to you. And again, I have no business here, so as soon as the sun is back in the sky, I'm on my way. You'll never have to see me again or worry about me throwing what you say in your face." She pointed out. "Sometimes it helps to say things out loud. Let me be listen to your woes in exchange for you not ripping my throat out."

"You know, we really aren't that type of beast. We only fight when necessary and we only take what is necessary, what we need to survive. People act like wolves are out here ripping out throats and killing for sport. We don't do that, we're not like vampires. Hell, if we were, those witches would have put us on a leash a long time ago."

"I'm sorry. I didn't mean to offend you. But my offer still stands. If you want to talk, if you need someone to listen, I'm here." She returned to preparing for her camp. She didn't think the woman would hurt her.

"Yeah, okay. It's not like I can tell anyone else here how I feel."

"How do you feel?" Shanoai asked.

"I feel like I want to get the hell out of The Den. Just for a while, you know. Just so I can think without the pack. To hear my own thoughts and decide what I want for myself." She squatted and looked up at the moon. "You know, in a pack, every person has a role and not everyone gets to choose what their role is. Not everyone gets to say what they want for themselves and I damn sure don't."

"Sound tough, not being able to choose what you want for yourself." Shanoai had a lot of problems, but she never lost her choice. She could have left Waoli at any time, but her instincts told her to stay where she was.

"It is." The wolf nodded. "I'm tired of it. I really wish I could say that I was happy here, but I'm not."

"Why don't you leave? It's not unheard of. I know there are wolves who travel. They leave The Den and they come back when they need to, or they don't. What's different about you? Why can't you do that? You're out here now walking on your not-so-private path." Shanoai pointed out. "Just keep going, take a trip to clear your mind."

"I think about it, I do, but it's complicated for me. There is a system of responsibility that keeps me kind of chained to this place." She chuckled. "It's crazy how much I think about it. A vacation sounds amazing. I really wish I could roam, but for some of us, the ties that keep us here are stronger than others. There are many days when I am envious of the people who get to come and go as they please."

"Well, you're here now. We can hang out. Maybe it'll give you the break you need. It's not exactly leaving, but I'm not from The Den. I don't know what's happening there and honestly, I could use the distraction too, so you'd be helping me out as much as I would be helping you."

"You want to have some kind of strange fellows' sleepover and then go our separate ways?" The woman chuckled at the idea, but her expression said she was considering it.

"Yeah, why not? I honestly don't think I'm going to get any sleep tonight, anyway. This horse has gas and I swear the entire ride she was cutting ass." She frowned, and they both laughed after Liz snorted.

The wolf stood again and looked over her shoulder. "You are kind of funny, I guess. And I could definitely use the distraction."

"I'm happy to be your distraction." Shanoai pulled a bottle of water from her bag. "Do I at least get to know your name?"

"Just call me K." The she-wolf answered.

"K?" Shanoai nodded. "Nice to meet you, K. I'm Shanoai. But you can call me Shan."

"Shan. Nice. How do we do this sleepover thing?" K asked as she looked at Shanoai's singular cot.

"You've never had a sleepover?" Shanoai asked. "You know, just hang out with the girls, chat through the night?"

"I wasn't the most popular person growing up." K shrugged. "Not a lot of opportunities for stuff like that when people typically avoid you."

"Neither was I." Shan laughed. "First time I slept over with anyone was when I moved in with my girlfriend. I don't think that counts, though. It's been fifteen years and we're still sharing a bed."

"Well, that still counts for more than I know." K laughed.

"How about this? You just sit, join me in eating this lovely bag of mixed berries and we just see how it goes."

"Works for me." K sat across from Shanoai, who handed her the bag of berries. "Any razeberries in here?"

"Yeah, you like them?"

"Yes, I do, but they're hard to get here since they grow so close to Moon Hollow. No one really wants to go over that way if they don't have to."

"Yeah, I understand. That's why we transported the trees to Mosail. It's one small grove, but it produces a decent amount." Shanoai said. "Maybe you can do that here."

"Funny how one of the most avoided areas has the best fruits." K laughed and poured some of the mix into her hand.

Their conversation was awkward at first, but soon they were gabbing like old friends. K talked about her hard times cultivating relationships and Shanoai revealed how she felt like an outcast in her home.

In a matter of hours, the two shared more about themselves than they had with others in a long time. It was easy to do, considering they weren't planning on seeing each other again. Shanoai did eventually fall asleep against the tree, despite Liz's continuing farts.

"I'm coming with you." K said as soon as Shanoai woke up.

"What?" Shanoai asked, rubbing the sleep from her eyes. "What do you mean you're coming with me?"

"Shan, you're right. I need time away from home and a quick trip with you to Preciosa to see some pixies sounds fun. And hell, if anything hairy goes down, I'll be there to have your back. You know those pixies can be tricky." K shrugged. "I don't know. It might be good for me."

"Oh, uh." Shanoai stood up, realizing that the woman had on different clothes and a new satchel draped over her shoulder. She'd also braided her short her back out of her face. "You've already packed?"

"You don't want me to come," K sighed. "I get it. This was supposed to be a quick friendship and now I'm just inviting myself on your trip."

"No, it's not that. It's just I don't know how they're going to accept me." Shanoai admitted. "How do I explain showing up with a wolf?"

"I wouldn't be worried about that." K waved off the thought.

"You wouldn't?" Shanoai laughed. "That's a first. Usually, people are totally against going there."

"No, I mean, the wolves and the pixies don't have any bad blood. Besides, I've been there before. They already know me. Might actually make it easier for you to show up with a familiar face."

"You've been to Preciosa?" Shanoai frowned.

The pixies weren't known to be big on visitors and yet K spoke as if she had an open invitation.

"Yes, as a matter of fact, I have. I have a lot of responsibilities for my pack, just like you do for the Selective. Sometimes I'm made to go places and do things that I rather not be doing. But at least walking into Preciosa was fun." The she-wolf responded. "I swear it's like a party there all the time. Bright lights, parties, and everything is so colorful. It's likely the most advance city we have in Novia, with the way they blend magic and technology."

"You're a big fan of Preciosa, huh?" Shanoai sighed. "Well, if you want to come, I won't stop you."

"Excellent." K smiled.

"You want to ride?" Shanoai pointed to Liz, who neighed.

"I think I'll run along with you. No offense, but one night in the gas bubble of that horse was enough." K pinched her nose.

"Yeah, I get it." The seer's shoulder shook as she laughed at the pained expression on K's face.

Another aggressive fart from Liz punctuated Shanoai's laughter and the aerohorse threw her head back as if she were Queen of the world.

SIX

Before they took off, K undressed and handed her clothes to her new companion, who secured them to the horse. She watched in awe as K shifted form to a massive wolf with blue-gray fur. Shanoai hopped on the back of Liz and they took off.

She watched K closely as she ran beside them. She could tell that the woman had never felt so free before. It was something genuine and wild in the way she ran. Shanoai hadn't seen it before, a wolf free, with nothing holding her back.

K was actually doing something for herself and Shanoai connected with that desire even though this trip wasn't one of freedom and of choice for her. It was one that she somehow knew would change her entire life.

After two hours of running, they were at the gates of Preciosa. The Maliora stood proudly at the barrier, just as it had always been. Its petals closed to the world. Shanoai jumped down from Liz's back and handed K her clothing.

Once K dressed, they approached the Maliora and waited. Shortly after, the petals opened, revealing the brightly lit entrance to Preciosa, and four guards walked out.

"A seer and a wolf together?" The front guard questioned them, his head only coming to Shanoai's chest. The pixies were a short people, it only added to their temperament when encountering outsiders. "This is a first."

"Yeah, I know we're an unlikely pair." Shanoai shrugged.

"What are you doing here? What's your purpose?" He asked shortly, visibly annoyed by the guests at their door.

"Something tells me you already know why I'm here. The head of the Sukra doesn't send out guards without notifying the receiving party. Your queen is expecting me, isn't she?"

"Shanoai Angelus, that's you?" He frowned, as if he was expecting someone more impressive.

"That's me." She raised her hands and did a small bow.

"And Ke–" He looked at the wolf, who quickly cut him off as he said her name.

"Just call me K." The she-wolf gave him a firm look.

"As you wish. But why are you here?" The guard continued his questioning. "We knew of the seer, but no one said anything about a wolf."

"I'm just tagging along, you know. She stopped in my territory. I got a little nosey and here I am." K stepped forward, her presence imposing on the guard. "Are you telling me you're going to turn me away? I don't think your queen, or my alpha, would approve of that. It might make for some unsettling consequences for you."

The guard stiffened as he swallowed the lump in his throat. "Fine, whatever. This is getting old anyway."

He looked the two women up and down then huffed.

"What's getting old?" Shanoai asked.

"Preciosa is a place where people don't come. We know how the rest of the world thinks of us. You see us as the crazy paranoid pixies. I gotta say I prefer it that way." He smirked. "Because almost every other day now, there is someone else banging on the gates asking to see the queen. I miss the days when I got to sit here on my post watching the wind blow by."

"You had other visitors?" K asked. Who else would want to come there?

"Let me guess, a peacekeeper?" Shanoai chewed her lip. The Peacekeepers had confirmed her dreams. Maybe they were on the same path of trying to fix whatever was going wrong in their world.

"Yes. He came with a shadow walker. How did you know that?" The guard asked.

"As I said, my leader isn't sending me across the world without a little advance research." She lifted her chin. "We know they're on to something. We just don't know exactly what it is. Or at least I don't."

"Right, you seers and your vision." He looked at Liz. "The others will mind your horse. You follow me. As you stated, the queen is expecting your arrival, and it is not smart for us to keep her waiting. We need to get this over with so you can keep moving."

"You in a rush to get us out of here?" K asked.

"Let's just say that the gates are closing soon and they won't be opening for a while." He looked at the open petals. "I don't think you want to be caught inside when that happens."

"You're locking down the city? Why?" Shanoai asked as she handed off Liz's reins to the guard that approached her.

"You're a seer." He looked at Shanoai, then to K. "And if memory serves, you're a powerful wolf. I know you both are aware of what's happening out here."

"What's that?" K asked, leading him to possibly reveal something they weren't aware of.

"You mean to tell me you don't see the changes happening in the world around you?" He scoffed. "I find that hard to believe. You don't feel the shift in energy or smell the stench of change in the air?"

"I feel it," Shanoai said, hoping to get him to his point faster.

"Good, because whatever our queen has learned in recent weeks is serious enough to make her issue the order. Preciosa hasn't gone on lockdown in over three hundred years. Not even the threat of the dragons was enough to make that happen. After the seer leaves here today, this gate will close, and it will not open again until our queen sees fit."

"Well, I guess we better get in and get out." K slapped Shanoai on the shoulder. "I don't know about you, but I have no interest in an extended stay here."

"Excellent, let's go." The guard turned and walked into the city, leaving them to follow.

"What's his problem?" Shanoai asked as they walked down the narrow path.

"Oh, he's always had a stick up his ass." K said, then shook her limbs. "Dammit, I always forget about this. Why is it necessary to make us their size in here? It freaks my wolf out!"

"I don't feel anything." Shanoai frowned. "What are you talking about?"

"You don't feel your body shrinking to pixie size?" She frowned. "Oh, it must be because you're part pixie. It doesn't affect you the same way."

"Oh, I guess that makes sense." Shanoai never gave much consideration to the pixie side of her bloodline until this trip. For years, she felt no connection to the hidden city or their magic. It never dawned on her it would have actually altered her in any significant way. That was the thing of being a hybrid. The child was always raised by the mother's side and rarely connected to the father.

"Sorry, Shan. I didn't mean to bring up any negative feelings." K apologized when she saw the confliction in her companion's expression.

"No, it's fine." Shanoai said, then changed the topic. "I take it he knows your real name." She pointed to the guard that walked ahead of them.

"You caught that, huh?" K shook her arms more as the tingling sensation from shrinking wore off.

"Yes, I did. Don't worry, I won't ask you about it. I understand you want to keep your anonymity and I'm okay with it." Shanoai kept her head straight and her voice low. "Just promise me one thing."

"What's that?" K asked.

"Keep nothing from me that might get me killed. I don't think knowing your name will affect my ability to survive this trip. But if there's something I need to know about you, anything that might put me in danger, you let me know."

"If I think of anything, I will definitely let you know." K looked at her. "But if you want me to go back to The Den, I can. I understand that this is uncomfortable for you, especially after what the stiff back guard just told us."

"No, you don't have to go. This trip is a good thing for you. Don't ask me how I know, but I do." Shanoai smile. "Honestly, I enjoyed the little banter back there, and it's better than talking to Liz. She's not one for conversation."

"Great." K clapped her hands as they reached the end of the path that opened to the hidden city. "Well, something's telling me that the queen will not want me in the room when you have your conversation. While you do that, I have a few pals in the city. I'll go pop in and say hello while you do your thing. Meet you back at the gates when you're done."

"Are you sure?" Shanoai asked as the guard continued

walking, unconcerned that she was no longer following him. Maybe he wanted he to get lost in the city.

"Yes, I'll be fine. If I thought there was anything to worry about, I'd have to tell you, right? You made me promise." K smiled and tapped her finger on her temple. "I never break a promise."

"True." Shanoai sighed. "Okay, well, don't do anything crazy." The last thing they needed was K getting into trouble and the Pixie Queen deciding to lock them both up.

"Hey, even if this isn't an official trip for me, I still represent The Den. I will not cause any trouble here." The she-wolf said with a straight face. "I don't want news of my being here getting back home anyway."

"Okay, well I should catch up since he clearly isn't concerned with me." Shanoai pointed to the guard who hadn't stopped to check for her.

"Have fun!" K said and strolled away in the opposite direction.

Shanoai ran to catch up with her escort. As she did, she took in the city's magnificence. It was like being in an entirely new world. She'd always known that Preciosa was far more advanced than the rest of Novia. People often compared their blending of magic and technology to cities like Tokyo on Earth. She'd seen pictures of the earth city with tall buildings and bright lights. While Tokyo was an awe-inspiring place, it had nothing on Preciosa.

Tall building, lights, magic, and pixies that's what she saw. There were floating clouds that lit up carrying clubs that were bumping with dance music. The smell of berries and other fruits filled the air, calming away the anxiety she felt when she first arrived. The place was both exciting and completely relaxing and it made her never want to leave without seeing much outside of the path ahead of her.

"We're here." The guard spoke as she finally caught up to him just outside the onion shaped building layered with the pink leaves of their home.

"Queen's home," he turned to her. "I see K has decided not to stay with us on this part of the trip."

"No. You're just okay with her running around the city?" Shanoai asked the guard. "Thought you guys were strict about stuff like that."

"Some of our guests have more range than others." He said simply.

"Don't suppose I'll be able to get that kind of treatment."

"I wouldn't count on it." He shook his head and opened the teardrop shaped doors.

"Of course not." She muttered.

There was a lot more to K than Shanoai knew, and she would spend the rest of their time together trying to figure out what it was. Something was special about the wolf. Somehow, it felt like they were supposed to be together.

Shanoai considered the feelings she had since meeting K. The powerful pull of intuition leading her to keep the wolf by her side.

She didn't know why or how, but K had a part to play in the grand scheme.

The teardrop shaped opened to an interior that made Shanoai's breath catch in her chest. Eyes wide, she looked at the room that was unmatched to anything she'd ever seen. The moving lights and color from the walls bounced on her skin, and the pink floors. Her stomach growled at the smell of cookies and other baked treats, she looked around but saw none and was disappointed.

"Stay here." The guard spoke, leaving Shanoai to wait. To both sides of the waiting area were doors and on the left a pair of stairs that followed the wall. The guard disappeared through the doors to her right.

A few minutes later, he returned with a woman who smelled of the cookies Shanoai searched for. "She will take you from here."

"Thanks." Shanoai said as the guard went back out of the doors that exited to the city.

"This way," the woman said softly and ushered Shanoai to the stairs.

They climbed the steps to another set of double doors, an obviously preferred design element for the space. These were silver and adorned with blue and purple flowers. The petals of the flowers interlocked where the two doors met. The woman touched her hand to the center most flower and one by one, like a zipper, the petals released their hold.

The doors opened with a breathy whisper, and the woman indicated for Shanoai to move forward. With some hesitation, she stepped inside.

The small woman said nothing more before closing the doors behind Shanoai, leaving her in the room alone.

They decorated the inside of the queen's chamber with the same petals from the Maliora that guarded the city of Preciosa. The magic in the flower worked as another layer of protection for the queen. Shanoai wondered what would happen next. The room was cool, nothing special about the decorations, not much for her to take in.

She turned back to the door, thinking this was a waste of time, but then the petal positioned at the back of the room lowered, and behind it stood a beautiful woman with bright eyes and a warm smile.

She stood bathed in a golden light, with butterflies fluttering around her. Her skin was a deep mahogany, and she wore a beautiful dress layered with colors of the rainbow. She had her hair pinned up in a bun and adorned with crystals, a floating crown.

"Shanoai Angelus." the queen welcomed her. "It is so great to meet you finally."

"It's nice to meet you too." Shanoai paused. "You've been waiting for me longer than a few days, haven't you?"

"Your instincts are improving already. Yes, as a matter of fact, I have for quite some time now." Saxfy smiled as she stepped from the platform.

"Someone told you I will come." Shanoai continued.

64

"Correct again." The queen smiled.

"Who?" Shanoai wondered who could have foretold her arrival. Waoli possibly, but if she'd known, why would she have condoned the mistreatment of Shanoai for so long?

"Your mother did." Saxfy admitted. "It was a long time ago before you were even born, actually."

"You knew my mother?" Shanoai took a deep breath, suddenly wondering what information Saxfy could share with her. Few people knew her mother and if they did, they acted like they didn't. Ashamed by the seer who was with a pixie.

"Yes, I did. And I knew you would come to me, and I knew you would need my help." The queen walked over to Shanoai. "When the peacekeeper came to see me earlier this week, I knew you would be the next to visit. Shortly after, I got a message from Waoli."

"It was her vision?" Shanoai realized then that she never knew who convinced the Sukra that they should believe in Shanoai. She just assumed the peacekeeper's word was enough for them.

"Yes, she confirmed my suspicions. There are many people who have been waiting for the time when you would to realize your true place in this world, Shanoai." Saxfy said. "You are so close to that moment. I'm just happy I'll be around to see it happen."

"What are you talking about?" The seer frowned. Yes, she felt out of place in Mosail sometimes, but she never thought she didn't belong there. It was her mother's home. Despite her lack of power and influence, Shanoai wanted to be there, to be closer to the woman she'd never know.

"I'm talking about what's broken within you." Saxfy answered, her voice transforming into a warm touch that caressed Shanoai's face and arms.

"Broken? You mean my vision?" Shanoai shrugged away from the invisible touch. "I've been this way my entire life. I know there are people who expect me to be better, but this is who I am."

"Shanoai, that is not what I mean." Saxfy shook her head. "There is so much that you don't understand. Your parents didn't want it to be this way."

"Well, can you tell me what you do mean because I gotta say, I'm already pretty damn confused right now. Excuse me for my language."

"What I mean is that your vision is not what's broken. It's merely affected by what has been disturbed within you. It's the reason you could see the man in darkness. You saw him, didn't you? In your dreams?"

"How do you know that?" Shanoai asked. "Waoli would never tell you that. I may not know what is going on, but we do not speak about visions that are not our own. It's bad luck."

"You're right, she didn't tell me. As I said, your mother came to me. She knew what was to come even before you were born, before you were even conceived." Saxfy explained. "She saw your dreams, she saw you as you are now and she prepared for this moment."

"How could she possibly know this?"

"You are what we call destined, Shanoai. Some souls are chosen by the universe to exist for a specific purpose. You're one of those souls." The queen laid her hand on Shanoai's shoulder. "You wonder why people were upset that you did not have powers of your own. It's because your mother was immensely powerful. She had strength like no other and she used that to better the world. The woman was magnificence personified."

"And then here I come, a child with none of that." Shanoai said. "Yes, I've heard this story my entire life."

"I understand." Saxfy said with pity in her eyes.

"What now? I mean, is this why Waoli wanted me to come? So you could tell me about my destiny?" She felt frustrated, no less confused than she'd always been. "What's the point of this? How does this help anything?"

"No, Waoli doesn't know why you're here, only that you need to be." Saxfy said and the butterflies that danced around her head quickened their pace.

"So you know something about me that others don't." Finally, Shanoai would get what she came for.

"I do." The queen smiled. "I've been holding on to this information for so long."

"And I assume you want me here so you can tell me what that is." Shanoai nodded. "But you'd prefer I be gone before the lockdown?"

"That would be preferred, yes. You cannot do what you need to behind the gates of the Maliora." Saxfy turned away from Shanoai and walked to the wall to the right of the room. "But I will not be the one to tell you. What you need to know isn't something for you to hear from me."

"If not you, then who?"

"Follow me, please." She pressed her hand against the panel of the wall and with a release of pressured air it opened.

The queen led Shanoai from her main chamber through the hidden doorway into a small room. The room had three doors and the center door was silver, with an eye etched in black.

"I believe you have something that will help you open this door." Saxfy pointed to the center door. "No one can open it but you. Your mother designed it that way, or should I say your father did."

"What? My father. You know my father." Shanoai perked up. She knew her father was alive, and heard stories of him when she was younger, but she'd never met him. Her caregiver always told her he was too dangerous to pursue. When she got older, she couldn't admit that she was too afraid to try looking for him.

"I know your father, yes. He's a great man and hopefully one day you'll be able to meet him, but today is not about that. Today is about getting you ready for what's coming. You need to go through that door and you need to do whatever it takes to fix what's broken within. Because if you don't, and I hate to say this because it's so much to put on your shoulders, but if you don't, Novia and the world as we know it, will be in great danger."

"No pressure there." Shanoai nodded and pulled the small box that Waoli gave her out of her pocket. "I take it this is the key?"

"I'll leave you to it." The queen nodded, turned, and left Shanoai alone.

She held the box in her palm, examining it before instinct kicked in. She flipped the box holding the eye towards the door. The surface of the box warmed before a bright ray of light shot from the eye etched into the box to the one on the door. The beam continued in a quick burst until the door absorbed the light.

It glowed, humming with energy as the light spread across the surface. Shanoai watched, a feeling of hope rushing over her, when the door finally opened.

"Another invitation." Shanoai looked around the room at the other doors. They were still closed, and neither felt like they were meant for her. She took a deep breath, kissed the picture of Charlie she kept in her pocket, then walked through the door. What other choice did she have?

The room was dark at first, but warm. Like climbing into bed beneath a weighted blanket. It was a hug from a friend, one she didn't realize she needed. Shanoai relaxed and nearly forgot why she was there until she heard the voice.

"You've come." The soft voice spoke from the darkness. "Finally."

"Who's there?" Shanoai squinted trying to find the source of the voice in the dark room.

"You're just as beautiful as I imagined." A figure of a woman, outlined in light, was a blur at first. The woman took slow steps toward her and as she got closer, the light spread from around her, filling the room and giving Shanoai a better view of her.

"Why do I know you?" Shanoai said as the woman came into view. "You feel so familiar."

"You are stronger than you know, Shanoai. You may not remember me, but I've always known how powerful you would be."

The light finally touched her face and Shanoai saw herself reflected in this woman.

"Wait." Shanoai shook her head. "Mom?"

"Yes." The woman smiled, and the room brightened.

"How is this possible? You're dead." Shanoai took a step back from the apparition. "This isn't right."

"I died, yes. But like all things, my death was destined to happen. I, unlike most people, knew when my time would come, which meant we could take precautions to make sure I could be here for you during this time." Her voice melted Shanoai's heart.

"We? You mean you and my father?" She wiped the falling tears from her eyes. The emotional response was overwhelming.

"Yes." Her mother smiled. "Your father was so proud of our plan. Unfortunately, it meant leaving you without us, but it was the best way we could think to protect you."

"Okay." Shanoai raised her hands. "This is making my head hurt. I was told I had to come talk to Saxfy to find information. This is too much. You're dead, but standing in front of me. My father is alive, but can't be near me. How does any of this tie into what's going on now? Darkness threatens Mosail. What does that have to do with me?"

"It is a lot to process, I know." Her mother stilled. "Take your time."

"That's an understatement." Shanoai looked for a place to sit, but found none. Her legs felt like they would give out on her.

"You do not have to understand it all right now. That is not the purpose of your time here." Her mother reasoned.

"Right, you're supposed to help me fix my vision, right?" Shanoai nodded. "Or at least whatever is broken inside of me that will help fix my vision."

"Yes, that is the goal." She smiled.

"How do we do that?" Shanoai asked. "We should get this done so I can get back to Mosail to help out."

"We don't do it here." Her mother responded. "There is a woman. Her name is Keyloa. She is the only one who can help you."

"Keyloa?" Shanoai frowned, not recognizing the name.

"Yes, she is a siren."

"A siren?" Shanoai laughed. "This just keeps getting better and better, doesn't it? I mean, first they send me to the land of the pixies, and now to the sirens. The sirens, who by the way, hate seers."

"Did they tell you this journey would be an easy one?" Her mother challenged her. "Were you promised a simple task that would fix everything?"

"They didn't tell me anything about what this journey would be, just that I had to take it or all of Novia would suffer." Shanoai admitted.

"With a warning like that, I'd think you'd realize that this would be a tough road to travel." The light softened around her figure. "If all the world is at risk, saving it would never be easy. I know you may not want it to be this way, Shanoai, but you are meant to help keep this world safe. This is only the beginning for you."

"Yeah, I guess I was trying to avoid those context clues." Shanoai dropped her head. "You know, typically the people chosen to save the world are in their teens. I'm knocking on thirty-five and you all want me to run across the world, battling an unknown evil."

"What teenager do you know right now who would realistically be capable of doing anything of this magnitude? This isn't some young adult novel from Earth. Though I did enjoy a few of them when I was alive."

"What do I have to do when I find this Keyloa?" Shanoai gave in. There was no other choice. She cared about the world and the people in it. She couldn't turn her back on her task.

"You must go to her, ask that she sing you the leymusair. It is a song only she can sing, and she must sing it to you at Faerwai or it will not work."

"And here I thought it couldn't get any worse." Shanoai scoffed. "You want me to convince a siren to take me, someone she sees as a mortal enemy, to Faerwai? A place sirens avoid like the plague? How do you expect me to do that?"

"You're the resourceful type. I'm sure you can figure it out." Her mother nodded. "You're my daughter. If you've inherited anything from me, it's my ingenuity."

"Of course, is there anything else I should know?" Shanoai looked back at the door behind her. She didn't want to leave, but something was telling her she had to. The time to chat with her mother had come to an end.

"Yes, I'm coming with you." Her mother smiled.

"What? How?" Shanoai scoffed. "You're dead, remember? You're not really here."

"You have the box?" She pointed to the small box still in Shanoai's hand. "It took a lot for your father to plant that so Waoli would find it. He couldn't exactly walk into the city and hand it to her without heads."

Shanoai held up the box. "This?"

"Yes, that's the vessel that will carry me." She pointed to the walls of the room. "It's made of the same magic, only in a portable package."

"You'll have to excuse me because my brain just broke at

the thought of carrying my mother's ghost around in a box in my pocket." Shanoai lifted the box in question. "How exactly is that supposed to work?"

"Just open it and I go inside. Then I'll be there whenever you need me." Her mother answered simply.

"This gets more unbelievable with everything you say."

"There is one thing you need to be aware of." She spoke. "Once we leave this room, our time is limited. I cannot stay with you forever. This room could sustain my spirit for a hundred more years. That box, while made of the same magic, doesn't provide enough power to do the same. When we leave, the countdown starts."

"So, no catching up on all the years you've missed out on?" Shanoai's voice cracked with her grief.

"I think we can squeeze that in. I'd love to hear about Charlie."

"You know about her?"

"Hey, I didn't go through all this to sit here and not check up on you." She warmed. "Now open the box and let's get moving. I hear Saxfy is closing up this place soon, and I've been trapped in the pixie corner for far too long as it is."

"Right." Shanoai opened the box and pointed it at her mother. The same light that opened the door shot out, wrapped around her mother, and pulled her inside. "Nothing weird about that at all." Shanoai muttered as she left the room.

SEVEN

Shanoai left the queen's home without ever seeing her again. The small woman returned and escorted her to the golden doors, where the guard led her back to the gates. As they moved, she heard whispers of the lockdown. The pixies wanted her out of there.

Just as she reached the border wall where the path to the Maliora gate was, K strolled up laughing with a pixie who hugged her before walking away.

"Did you get what you need?" K asked as she waved off her friend. "We good to go now?"

"Yes. And I'll explain it to you later." Shanoai turned her eye to the pixie man, who hugged K and happily walked away. "You're really friendly with the pixies. I never would have believed it."

"Hey, I'm a sociable person, despite the claws." She spoke. "So, what's the next move?"

"Now I head to Sabrine." Shanoai admitted as they walked through the Maliora, where the other guards stood with Liz.

"Sabrine? Why would you want to go there?" K watched the guard closely. "I mean, I thought seers didn't exactly get along with sirens."

"We don't, but apparently I'm going to need the help of one." Shanoai responded. "I was naïve to believe that this trip would be a simple one."

"Oh?" K asked. "What made you think it would be simple?"

"I was told I had to come get something from the Pixie Queen. I did that. Now I'm told I need to go to Sabrine. That wasn't on the agenda when I left home." Shanoai said. "Something tells me that once I do what I need to in Sabrine, it's only going to get worse."

"Are you thinking of not going?" K asked. "We could always take a trip to Kilosh. The songbirds aren't the most welcoming, but they don't have any issue with seers."

"You mean defy a queen and go back to the head of my people from an incomplete journey?" Shanoai shook her head. "Besides, songbirds hate wolves."

"Not this wolf." K winked. "You let me know if you change your mind. We could just take off, you know." She added and pointed west. "Take off with the sun at our backs, never to come home again."

"What about your responsibilities back home?" Shanoai challenged the fantasy K presented. "And I have Charlie. I can't just leave her behind. She's my world. There's no way I would ever be happy without her."

"Dammit, you're right." K chewed her lip. "There are people back home I'd like to see again too."

"Look, I know wolves have just as much issue with sirens as we do. You don't have to keep going, K." Shanoai said. "I appreciate you coming, but I don't know where this leads."

"You're right, we have our issues, but..." K looked back in the direction of The Den.

"But?"

"I'm coming with you," K announced firmly. "This trip isn't over. You're not getting rid of me yet."

"K, this could be dangerous." Shanoai warned again.

"I can't go back, Shan." She looked at the seer with a sort of hopeless look. "I get it, it can be dangerous. But I can't go back there. Not yet. I can't. So please don't make me."

"You were looking to get away so you could clear your mind. This isn't exactly a vacation."

"No, it's not, but it's what I want to do. For once, I'm doing what I want to do. Don't ask me why I want so badly to help a seer, but I do. And it feels good to decide for myself. Besides, nothing will take my mind off my problems at home better than the potential face off against sirens."

"We aren't going there for a fight, you know?" Shanoai shook her head. "I need their help and something tells me if you wolf out, they will not be in the helping mood."

"I know, I know. But a girl can dream." She teased. "So I say we get out of here before we get trapped inside. Besides, I'm sure Liz is ready to get out of here."

"I think it's the pixies who are ready for her to go." They laughed, looking over at the guard, who looked sickly.

"What the hell have you been feeding her?" K asked. "I've never heard of a gassy horse before."

"Oh, don't blame this on me." Shanoai denied the accusation. "They gave Liz to me before I left. I guess she was the only horse no one would miss."

"Despite her funk, I like her. She's got character." K boasted. "Every good companion needs some, especially on a trip like this."

"You're right. I'd still prefer the kind of character that doesn't require a gas mask." Shanoai laughed as Liz let a big one rip and the guard gagged.

"So, we're off to Sabrine." K repeated as they grabbed Liz, exited the Maliora, and the petals pulled in, sealing the city off yet again.

"Yes, and we need to get going. It's a long ride around Celest Lake." Shanoai rubbed Liz's neck.

"We could always cut our time," the she-wolf suggested. "The bridge is still intact last I checked. We could cross over Celest Lake instead of going around it."

"This journey is hard enough. Let's not add a water dragon to the list of things we need to face." Shanoai rejected the suggestion.

"Yeah, you're right. Let's not push our luck."

They traveled along the coast of Celest Lake, close enough to cut their time, but not enough to tempt the dragon within. As the sun set, they stopped to find a place to rest. Just outside the Warped Forest where there was enough cover from potentially being seen by the nearby dragons. There was also enough food for foraging.

K ran off on her own two feet. Berries and herbs weren't enough for a wolf who'd run for over a day. By the time she returned to Shanoai, the seer had already put their camp together and taken care of Liz.

"So now that we're away from the pixies, you want to fill me in on the details?" K cleaned herself up using the rest of the water she'd collected from a nearby stream.

"You want the long story or the short one?"

"Give me the short and simple." She yawned. "Not sure how much longer I'll be able to keep my eyes open."

"Right. So long story short, years before I was born, my mother left a message with the queen. There is a way to fix what's broken inside of me. She said the problem is deeper than just not having vision."

"And the answer to this problem is in Sabrine?" K asked.

"Yes, apparently the only way to fix me is to hear a song sang by a siren," Shanoai laughed as she popped another berry in her mouth. "I guess it works as some sort of key."

"Well, that's not so hard, right? Just have to get them to let us inside." K noted as she sipped her water. "Shouldn't be too hard to do that."

"The song has to be sung on Faerwai." Shanoai added.

K burst out laughing. Spitting the water in her mouth out, which sprayed the seer in the face.

"Really?" Shanoai wiped the water from her face.

"Sorry," K said, still snickering.

"You're sorry, but you're still laughing." She threw a berry at her.

"I'm sorry." She held her side. "But that's messed up. How are you supposed to do that? It's like siren anti-matter over there, right? I don't exactly know what happens to them when they get there, but it changes them."

"I don't know what I'm going to do, but I'm hoping this Keyloa already knows I'm coming, and I won't have to do too much convincing. Because this shit is bad enough as it is."

"Well, whatever the plan is, I need to get some rest." K yawned. "We still have almost another day of running ahead of us."

"Sounds good." Shanoai took out the picture from her pocket and stared at the face of her wife.

"You going to reach out to Charlie?" K asked. "I know you must have some magical form of communication. I heard about those echo devices you use."

"I have one, yes, but I can't reach out to her right now. It could be dangerous. Rule number one of our trainings. When you're in the field, you focus on the goal. Calling home could be a senseless and costly mistake."

"Shan, you going to be, okay?" K watched Shanoai closely.

"Yeah," Shanoai put the picture back in her pocket. "I'll be home soon enough. Get some sleep."

The next day, they got up, ate, and carefully collected more water for the trip. As they packed up their things and the she-wolf handed Shanoai her clothes, they heard it. An enormous explosion that came from the west. K touched the ground, feeling the shock that ran deep beneath the surface.

"What the hell was that?" K looked over her shoulder towards the source of the sound. "Did you feel that?"

"I don't know, but I'm not about to go investigate it." Shanoai secured the bags on Liz. "That's someone else's problem. We have enough on our plate as it is."

"Smart. Let's keep moving." K started her shift, but stopped when the sounds of dragons crying rang out.

Just above the top of the trees, they saw them. Four dragons took to the sky, shooting off in four different directions.

"That's not a good sign, is it?" K looked at Shanoai.

"No, I don't think it is." She shook her head.

"Where do you think they're going?" K asked.

"Hell, if I know. But as I just said, we have enough to worry about." Shanoai hopped on Liz's back. "Let that be someone else's problem."

"Fine by me." K said, then shifted into her wolf.

They started their run, leaving the mystery behind. Their path took them through the outskirts of the Warped Forest and past the border wall of Havenpoint, the city of refugees. Just beyond the place of last resort was one of the many siren ports. Sabrine.

"Ah, my ass hurts." Shanoai groaned and rubbed the kink out of the back of her leg after hopping down from Liz's back.

"Two days on a horse will do that for you." K said as she pulled her shirt back on. "We could have got here faster if we took the bridge, you know."

"Right, I didn't hear you volunteering to fight off the dragon two days ago." Shanoai pointed out as she made sure Liz was comfortable. "Good thing this place is flush with razeberries. Liz loves them."

"You know that could be why she keeps stinking up the place." K pointed at the pile of berries. "That stuff is full of sugar. You should put her on a better diet. One that won't blow her stomach up."

"As I said, Liz isn't my horse. When we get back to Mosail, she goes back with the others in the Cisk stables. I'm just making sure she is good and survives this trip. Gas ass and all."

They left Liz under tree cover with enough food and water. They did not tie her down because aerohorses never needed to be restrained. As long as they were comfortable, they wouldn't go anywhere.

Sabrine was a coastal city, the entrance marked by a massive ship split in half that sat on the beach. As they approached, two women stepped out of the wreckage.

They were beauties, both of them. One with a thin muscular frame, long dark hair, and big brown eyes. The other was curvy, shorter, with purple hair cut in a bob and light brown eyes.

They observed their unknown visitors. Keeping a close watch on the wolf. If they thought K was there to do any harm, they would sound the alarm.

"You think they're going to be nice about this?" K asked in a hushed tone.

"Yeah, right." Shanoai rolled her eyes.

"What are you doing here?" The taller woman asked as she adjusted the nose ring. It had a small chain that linked to the hoop in her earlobe.

"I'm here to see a friend." Shanoai answered her.

"A friend? What friend does a seer have in Sabrine?" The other asked, disgusted by the idea.

"Her name is Keyloa." Shanoai gave the name her mother told her. "She is expecting me."

"Keyloa is expecting you?" She laughed, hitting the other woman on the arm. "You believe this?"

"No, I don't. But I say let them try their luck." She shook her head. "How long do you think they'll survive?"

"That depends on how frisky the loner is feeling today. Keyloa isn't the nicest of our kind and she damn sure ain't friends with a seer or a wolf."

"Maybe not," Shanoai chimed in. "But Saxfy says she is."

"Saxfy? As in—"

"The Pixie Queen, yeah." K answered. "You think that might have a little influence over Keyloa's decision-making?"

"You're lying." The purple-haired siren said. "Why would the queen send you here? You come here with a lot of claims and no proof."

"People will say anything to get through these gates. How do we know you aren't lying?" The other added.

"Okay, we'll just leave," Shanoai said. "And when we do, they'll send someone else, someone who will come with more force. Then you can explain why you turned us away. How well do you know the Cisks? I'm sure they will be happy to pay you a visit."

"Let them through." The tall siren relented. "It's not worth the headache."

"You can't be serious." Her partner griped. "Just like that?"

"I'm not dealing with the wrath of the pixies or any fucking Cisks. It's not worth it. If they want to talk to Keyloa, let them. If they aren't legit, she'll deal with it."

"Fine." She nodded. "You go straight to Keyloa. No detours. We will be watching. You step out of line, and you get your asses tossed out. Understood?"

"Perfectly." Shanoai smiled.

They turned to the wreckage and sang. Their voices blended to form the key that opened their world. The air between the two sides of the ship rippled and what looked like the beach meeting the ocean changed. The city of Sabrine stood before them, full of life, music, and the descendants of the sea.

"As much as I don't like them, I have to admit that's pretty damn cool." K said with a soft sigh.

"Yeah, it is." Shanoai agreed.

"Go on," the short one pointed. "Stay on the path and you will find her."

"You think you can give us a little more to go off than that?" K asked. "Not as if either of us knows where we're going."

"I'd think friends of Keyloa would know where her house is." She smirked.

"You see that large ominous-looking house right there?" The tall siren pointed to the furthest house on the path. "That's the home of your dear friend Keyloa."

"Of course, it is." Shanoai said. "Why would I expect anything but the haunted house to be our destination?"

"Have fun." She said as the gate rippled and closed behind them.

EIGHT

"What, no escort?" K called out as they were sealed inside of the city. "You know I heard sirens had poor manners, but that's just rude."

"Did you hear that?" Shanoai looked back at the gate.

"What?" K asked.

"They're laughing at us." Shanoai looked like she wanted to fight.

"Wouldn't you be? I mean, we're in a place we don't know, walking to what looks like the worst house on the block, and probably going to be poisoned or sang to death by some pissed-off siren. From their perspective, it's hilarious."

"You'll have to excuse me if I don't see the humor in this situation right now." Shanoai balled her fist at her side. "I just want to get this over with so I can go home."

"Ah, you will, one day, when we're old and gray and looking back on this moment." K touched Shanoai's shoulder. "Calm down, girlfriend. We don't want to show up on Keyloa's doorstep angry. I doubt that will help convince her to do what we need."

"Good to see you planning for the future." Shanoai looked at K.

"It's nice to think about, from time to time." She winked. "Hopefully, there's a hunky wolf in mine. The kind that waits on me hand and foot."

Despite getting the stamp of approval to be inside the city, Shanoai and K were on edge as they walked through the small city to get to Keyloa's house. Everyone inside looked at them like they'd crawled from the bowels of hell.

Even though K said she found the humor in their situation, Shanoai could tell that the wolf was just as much on the edge as she was. And for good reason. They kept to the path as they were told, a path that led straight down the middle of the city full of sirens.

No one approached them, but they watched the two women closely. A few sang soft songs, a melodic warning. If the wolf or the seer stirred up any trouble, they would pay for it. The collective song of sirens could be dangerous if they wanted it to be. It was a sound that could scramble a person's brain.

"And Keyloa's supposed to be the tough one?" K muttered. "It's not as if the rest of them are so welcoming."

"Did you expect them to be?" Shanoai asked. "We knew when we came here how they would receive us."

"No, I guess not." K kept a watchful eye on those they passed by. "They could at least pretend. That's what we do when we have unwanted guest. We make them feel welcomed and then, if they step out of line, we rip their throats out."

"Yes," Shanoai chuckled. "Give them a false sense of comfort first. Better way to go."

"Hey, it works for us."

They made it to the end of the path to the large house that looked like something made more for a pirate than a siren. Dark wood stood in stark contrast with the rest of the city done in tones of blue and green. Whoever Keyloa was, she wasn't someone who cared about standing out.

Shanoai climbed the steps to the house and knocked on the door. She waited but there was no answer. She tried again and again got no answer.

"What now?" K asked.

"I don't know, we can just wait for her to get back. Maybe she is out shopping or…" Shanoai started.

"Calling men to their death at sea?" K said with a spooky tone.

"Well, yeah, she could be doing that too." Shanoai shrugged.

"I–" K started, but stopped suddenly, eyes and ears alert.

"What is it?" Shanoai looked around, knowing the she-wolf could hear and see things she couldn't.

"There is someone behind the house." K said.

"Think it could be her?"

"This doesn't seem like a place that gets many visitors." The wolf pointed out. "I say we go check it out."

Shanoai nodded and descended the stairs, with K following closely behind her. They walked around the back of the house carefully. As they rounded the house that sat close to the water, they saw a figure coming out of the sea. She had translucent skin that shimmered with the light of blue and purple, but as the water dripped from her body, she changed.

The webbing between her fingers split and the raised ridges at her collarbone and cheeks flattened and faded into soft brown skin. Her hair, which was a soft gray, turned jet black and as she moved further from the water, it shrank into a tight afro that framed her face.

"Keyloa? Is that you?" Shanoai called out from a safe distance just in case they needed to run from the siren.

"Who wants to know?" She looked up, then tilted her head to the said as she examined her visitor. "Seer?"

"And a wolf." K waved as she stepped from behind Shanoai.

"What are you doing here?" Keyloa asked unphased.

"Saxfy sent us." Shanoai answered.

"Lorilei Angelus." She nodded, saying Shanoai's mother's name. "Always said her favor would come, even after her death."

"Well, here I am."

"What do you want me to do?" Keyloa asked. "Half a century since your mother came to me. So I assume whatever you want has to be major. You are her daughter, aren't you? You look just like her."

"I need you to sing the leymusair." Shanoai cut to the chase.

"That's it?" She shrugged. "I can do that, just give me a minute to get dressed."

"It's not that simple. It has to be done at Faerwai." Shanoai said, stopping her.

"Excuse me?" Keyloa turned back to them, throwing her hand on her hip. "Did I hear you correctly?"

"It has to be done there. It's the only way this works." Shanoai repeated. "I know it's a lot to ask, but that's what she said."

"Do you know what could happen to me if I go there?" Keyloa cocked her head.

"In theory," K responded.

"In theory, it could make me lose my fucking mind." Keyloa clarified. "Sirens who go there rarely come back the same. They turn into messed up monsters who lose themselves in the voices inside their mind. Most never recover from it. Those who do, well, they aren't hanging around places like Sabrine."

"Look, I wouldn't ask if it wasn't necessary," Shanoai

explained. "There is something broken inside of me. Something that can apparently only be fixed with your voice on that island." She pointed in the distance to where the fire red island sat in the sea.

"Something broken inside of you." Keyloa scoffed. "You really have some nerve coming here. You're broken, you can live on being broken. Going there could kill me!"

"Will you take me?" Shanoai asked.

"No." Keyloa said plainly. "Find another siren willing to risk her life for you."

"What do you mean, no? You owe a favor." K challenged the siren. "You going back on your word?"

"A favor yes, but that is no simple favor. I never said I would lay my life on the line."

"If you don't, you'll be putting all of Novia on the line." K stepped forward. "Is that someone you want on your shoulders?"

"How could that be true? The world will crumble if I don't take a seer to Faerwai?" She scoffed. "Give me a break."

"Look, I don't like it any more than you do. But this is what I was told. If not, I wouldn't be here." Shanoai admitted. "They have to think it's a pretty big deal to have sent me here."

"They?" Keyloa asked. "Who are they?"

"Waoli, Saxfy, and my mother." Shanoai said. "This is where

92

the journey leads. To you and to that island, however much I may wish it didn't."

"Three powerful beings told you that if I don't sing the leymusair to you on Faerwai, the world would be at stake?" Keyloa asked.

"Basically, yes."

"Fuck." She paced the sandy ground. "I can't believe this is actually happening."

"I take it that's enough to convince you?" K asked.

"I thought that old bat was crazy." Keyloa said. "You know, just some old woman trying to scare a kid into doing something she didn't want to. I didn't want to spend hours learning this stupid song."

"What are you talking about?" Shanoai frowned as she watched the pacing siren.

"When I was younger, a woman visited me. She smelled like a seer, but she was something different, something ancient, you know." Keyloa took a deep breath as she recalled what happened. "She told me to learn the song. There aren't many who know it and fewer who can sing it accurately. This woman was adamant that I learn it. It had to be me. Not my sisters or anyone else.

"She told me if I didn't learn it, bad things would happen to my family. So of course I killed myself spending years learning the damn thing, only to never see that woman again. Nothing ever happened. No one asked me to sing the song and my family was fine. I thought she was just crazy."

"But you learned it." Shanoai wanted clarity.

"I did." Keyloa said. "It cost me so much to learn it. Friends and family thought I was crazy for practicing the song. I hurt people, you know."

"What?" Shanoai asked. "Who did you hurt?"

"The leymusair has to be practiced on someone. That's the only way you know if you did it right. If you do, it's life changing for the person it's intended for. And if you get it wrong, well, you can destroy the very fabric of their being."

"You destroyed someone with this song?" K asked. "That's reassuring."

"Yes, well mostly animals, but there was someone–" She stopped. "It doesn't matter now."

"Now you know she wasn't crazy. What she said was true." Shanoai said. "You said you hurt people to learn this song. Are you going to tell me you did that for nothing?"

"Dammit." Keyloa stopped pacing. "Fine."

"You'll take me?"

"Yes," she huffed. "Not like I have a choice in the matter. If what you say is true, the world depends on it. I already have enough shit on my conscious."

"Great, let's go!" K cheered.

"You can't go." Keyloa held her hand up.

"What?" K frowned. "Why not?"

"Sorry, but no, this song is only to be heard by the intended. You can't go. Unless you want to end up with your mind twisted."

"What do you expect me to do, just stay here?"

"I don't know, hang out, go for a swim, I don't care." She turned, heading for the water. "Let's get this over with. It's best if we do this at night. Your connection to the moon will help make this easier on your mind."

"Yeah, you two just go ahead." K complained. "I'll hang out here, no problem."

"Hey, you wanted a vacation." Shanoai commented as she watched Keyloa head back to the water.

"Right, beachside with angry sirens nearby. Could anything be more relaxing?" The wolf threw her hands up in the air.

"I hope you're a good swimmer." Keyloa commented as Shanoai joined her.

"Best in class." She said proudly.

"Let's hope that counts for something. Stay behind me and you'll be fine." Keyloa instructed. "You can ride the current. It will make it easier for you. We don't have a lot of time and it's almost three miles away."

"Couldn't we take a boat?"

"We're sirens." Keyloa held her arms out, gesturing to the coastline where not one boat was in sight. "What boat would you like us to take?"

"Oh, right. Okay." Shanoai undressed to her underwear, leaving her clothes on the beach with a grumpy wolf who would eventually find her way into Keyloa's stash of spirits.

Shanoai swam directly behind Keyloa like she told her to. The force of the siren cut through the water, leaving a smooth trail that eliminated the resistance for Shanoai. She swam as hard as she could to keep up with the siren.

They made it to the island, and Keyloa immediately started moving. Shanoai, however, became mesmerized by the island. The light pink sand peppered with bright red crystals covered the ground. The further they walked, the more crystals she saw.

"What do you know about this place?" Keyloa asked as she moved carefully across the sand.

"Not much, outside of the fact that it can change a siren into something dark." Shanoai admitted.

"You should know more. That way you won't get us into any trouble." Keyloa paused. "The reason that this place can change a siren into something dark is because of the hastios crystals. They cover the ground, but the ones that cause the most trouble are up there."

She pointed ahead to where a huge formation of crystals shot up into the sky.

"So we avoid those?" Shanoai nodded.

"That would be preferred, but to do what you want, we have to go right into the heart of them."

"What?" Shanoai's eyes widened. "But that means you could—"

"Turn very dark. Yes, so listen to me now." She hardened as she looked Shanoai in the eye. "Touch nothing and don't even think about taking one of those crystals home with you."

"Okay."

"I mean it. Everyone always thinks sirens are crazy when we say this, but if you take one of these home, you're going to bring hell down on anyone you come in contact with."

"Okay, I got it." Shanoai put her hands up. "Look I'm naked with nowhere to store a crystal. I'm not planning on taking anything with me."

"Good, because as dangerous as it is for me, it's worse for someone with vision. Even with broken vision." Keyloa turned and continued to walk.

"What do you mean?" Shanoai asked as she tiptoed around a large crystal, afraid to disrupt it.

"These crystals affect those of us who are connected to the moon. Sirens depend on its power for the tides. Seers pull power direct from the moon, for its predictive nature. We don't know why, but for us, these crystals can be toxic." They continued walking. "When we get in there, move carefully, touch nothing. Hopefully, we both can get out of here alive. We only have a couple of hours left until the moon is above us. It's best if we do it then."

Shanoai followed Keyloa into the cluster of crystals that reached at least fifty feet in the sky. Some areas were easier to navigate, others not so much as the pathways varied in size from two feet to ten feet. It made it very difficult for them, but they made it.

The moon was moments from its peak as they made it to the center of the crystals. The light filled the cluster, quickly bouncing between the surface of the crystals and creating a kaleidoscope effect. Shanoai looked at her hands as the colorful spectrum danced across her flesh.

"Stand there in the center." Keyloa pointed to the spot just beneath the center of the stones, where it opened to the sky. "We only have a few minutes to get this done. I'm going to sing this song and I need you to focus on how it makes you feel, let it resonate with you. If you avoid it, if you fight its effect, it will not work. If it doesn't work, this will have been a total waste of time. I don't know about you, but I'm not trying to risk my life by coming here again."

"I understand." Shanoai nodded.

"Good." Keyloa looked up at the sky. "It's time."

The siren stood beneath the moonlight as it reached over them. She relaxed her shoulders, dropped her head back, and called to the voice within her. As she connected with her inner being, her skin returned to its translucent state, a rainbow effect dancing just beneath the surface, making her presence hypnotic.

Her voice started low, vibrating through the space and rose in tone until it reached up into the sky. The sound was melodic, hypnotic and as it bounced around them, echoing off the stones, it created a visible wavelength that shot directly into Shanoai's chest.

Shanoai held herself steady as the voice of the Keyloa reached into her, looking for that which was broken. It was invasive and made her tremble. There was no way to resist the feeling, no way to fight the vulnerable way it made her feel.

Tears ran down her face and she sobbed for all the sadness that it pulled up from within her. It was every part of herself that she ever denied and every hope that she ever had to throw away. It reminded her of every time she got her hopes up for something better, dreamed for something more for herself, only for it to be rejected. Everything dark and painful came back to her.

The feeling of complete and total helplessness took her over until she felt so deep in the darkness that she didn't know if she could come out of it again. But then it changed. Bringing light back into her world. Shanoai reached out to that light, hoping to understand what it was.

It was the love and acceptance she got from Charlie. The feeling of hope and promise when they confessed their love for each other. She felt more of that with the memory of her first rejected vision. It was the confidence she'd lost after being told all her life that she was the broken seer. Even though that vision wasn't a full one, it made her feel better about who she was.

Soon after was the feeling of excitement, thrill, and adventure when she met K. Despite the situation they were in, they had fun. Suddenly she couldn't deny that though there was bad in her life, there was so much good, so much worth fighting for.

And then she thought of her mother, the one and only time she saw her face and it made everything worth it because she knew that her mother was proud. She loved her, no matter what. And as that feeling of love stretched across her heart, the light from the moon shot down, filling the crystals with this energy and it passed through them into her.

Shanoai heard the voice of their goddess. This was what she expected the first time around. To feel the power of something more than herself. It was the way the other seers described it. Shanoai welcomed her goddess into her heart and she allowed that which was broken to be mended.

She felt herself becoming whole for the first time. When Keyloa ended her song, Shanoai stood there with tears streaming down her face and a smile that told of the love she felt.

"Did it work?" Shanoai asked as she looked at Keyloa.

"I don't know, do your eyes usually glow like that?" Keyloa stepped closer and her skin shifted back to the warm brown.

"Glow?" Shanoai asked. "No, what do you mean?"

"Yes, it's as if the moon is living inside your eyes. It's beautiful." Keyloa pointed to Shanoai's reflection on the side of the crystal. "See?"

"This is amazing." Shanoai leaned closer to the crystal, but Keyloa pulled her back before she got too close.

"Careful, remember this stuff is dangerous." Keyloa warned. "How do you feel?"

"I feel amazing. I mean, that was..." She looked back up at the siren. "I can't explain what that was."

"Well, glad it worked. Now we need to get out of here." Keyloa looked nervous. "Remember, touch nothing."

"Got it." Shanoai nodded.

They made it out of the crystals and to the beach. But as they headed back into the water, Shanoai fell to her knees, her eyes glowing with the light of the moon. She no longer saw the sand or the sea. And for the first time in her life, she saw a clear vision.

This was not of a dark figure wrapped in shadows, it was something else. She saw a man, a shadow walker, returning home to retrieve something important. As he exited his home, those in golden cloaks appeared with a goal of stopping him from continuing on his journey. She saw him fighting for his life and then there was something else, something no other seer had ever explained happening.

She heard a voice that addressed her. Inside the vision, there was something there that guided her, telling her what to do with this information. The voice told her she had to do something; she had to stop this event from happening.

"Are you okay?" Keyloa dropped to the sand besides Shanoai. "What's going on?"

"I..." Shanoai shook her head. "I had a vision."

"So soon?" Keyloa looked almost proud of herself. "I guess we can say it worked."

"Yeah, I need to go. There is something happening that need to stop." Shanoai got back to her feet, touching her forehead.

"Hell, I'm not looking to stay here any longer than I need to. You good to swim back?"

"Yes, let's go."

They swam back to the shores of Sabrine, this time faster as Shanoai moved ahead of Keyloa. She wasn't sure if it was her mother's blood or her father's, but she found a new ability underneath the water. Now connected to the moon and the goddess, she tapped into that power to create an underwater current that pushed her faster and further than she could ever do on her own.

"That was fun!" Shanoai said she stepped from the water.

"I think that song did a little more than fix your vision." Keyloa took a deep breath. "I could barely keep up with you."

"Thank you," Shanoai called out. "You have no idea what this means to me."

"Yeah, well, the favor is done. Please don't come back here asking me to do anything else like this."

"You're back!" K called out. "Thank god, I was losing my mind here."

"Tired of life on the beach already?" Keyloa smirked.

"Yes, I'm over it." She squinted as she addressed Shanoai. "Are you okay? There is something different about you."

"It worked." Shanoai said. "I've already had my first vision."

"Really? What was it?" K looked like she would cheer from her excitement. "Where are we going next?"

"I saw a man in his home and Cisks there. They were attacking him." The seer reported. "I need to stop that from happening. I have to defend that man."

"Cisks, as is the guardians from Mosail." K asked. "You have to fight your own people?"

"Yes, but there was something else, something different."

"What was it?" K asked.

"When a seer has a vision, it's just that, a vision of what may come. If it's something big, they will take it to the Sukra to decide on what to do with what they saw. This was different, this was more." Shanoai told her. She needed to say it out loud because it made no sense to her.

"How was it different?" Keyloa asked, picking up a towel from the bench beneath her house to dry her skin.

"I saw what happened and then, I heard a voice." Shanoai said.

"A voice?" Keyloa stopped. "What voice?"

"I don't know who or what it was. But it told me I have to stop this from happening and it left me with this intense feeling. Whatever is coming, it's bad, and it's tied to this event."

"So where is this vision leading us?" K asked as she sipped from the drink she held in her hand. Neither Shanoai nor Keyloa realized she had it, but when the siren saw it, she frowned.

"You've been in my home?"

"Oh, I hope you don't mind. I got so parched out here in the sun." K grinned around the mouth of the bottle.

"Mutt," Keyloa muttered.

"We're headed to Moon Hollow." Shanoai blurted out before K could say anything else. They were dancing on thin ice with their bickering.

"You're serious right now?" K asked and swirled the bottled in the air.

"Yes, and again, if you don't want to go, I understand."

"Nope, I'm coming." K looked at Keyloa and frowned. "You got something in your hair there."

"What?"

"You mind?" K walked over and picked a sliver of red and held it in her hand.

"Fuck," Keyloa blanched.

"That's not good, I take it." K dropped the piece in Keyloa's hand.

"No, it's not." Keyloa's face turned red with anger. "Now if you can get out of here I have to try to stop my life from falling apart."

"I'm sorry," Shanoai tried to apologize, understanding why Keyloa was upset. The sliver in her hair was a piece of crystal. The same crystal she warned Shanoai to be careful of.

"Save it." She held up her hand and stomped off toward the house. "Just get the hell out of Sabrine."

"You really enjoy getting into trouble, don't you?" K asked as they started their walk back to the city border.

"Trust me, it's not my choice. I'd much rather be sitting on the beach like you were." Shanoai pointed to the drink K still nursed. "I suppose you didn't think to get me one?"

"Nope." K took the last of the drink to the head and tossed the bottle aside. "Well, when you do take your vacation, make sure you pick a different beach because this one was no fun."

"You didn't enjoy the shore?" Shanoai raised a brow.

"They kept coming to watch me. Swimming by like I was some artifact on display." K shook her head. "I swear they were acting like I was going to shift and run along the shore to give them a show."

"Sounds voyeuristic." Shanoai laughed. "Maybe you should have."

"Ugh, don't make it worse than it already is." K looked

disgusted.

"You could have put on a little show for them." Shanoai slapped the wolf on the shoulder. "Shake a little tail."

"Next time, I'll be sure to do a little wolf dance for them." K winked. "Maybe they would have fed me. I'm starving and the evil one had no grub."

"You come here and disrespect our home?" A woman called out behind them and both Shanoai and K turned to see the woman, who wore a sheer dress stomping up behind them.

"What?" Shanoai asked, confused by what she claimed.

"Look around, we respect our land." The woman yelled, and as she spoke others appeared, following her. "We let you in our home and you have no respect for it."

"K, what did you do?" Shanoai looked over at the wolf, who already wore a guilty look.

"I just tossed the bottle." K admitted. "Sorry, I didn't think about it."

"Dammit, K."

The woman pointed at the outsiders and as the others joined her, their voices grew in anger as they spoke of capturing and torturing the women.

"I think it's time to run." Shanoai suggested.

They ran, covering their ears with their hands as they put distance between them and the forming mob. If the sirens started to sing, they would take over the two women, and they'd have no chance of getting away.

Shanoai felt hopeful that they could outrun the sirens, but when they reach the city's edge, she realized they could go no further. The gate to Sabrine was still closed and the two guards who let them in stood proudly watching over their post. The short one smirked as K and Shanoai came to a halt. They had no plans to open the gate.

"Fuck." K looked behind them. The mob was quickly approaching. "What now?"

"Look, you have let us out of here." Shanoai said. "We can't stay here."

"Or what?" The short woman looked happy to see them panic. "We told you not to step out of line. Why shouldn't we punish you for your sins?"

"Sins? I dropped a bottle. Call me a liter bug, but it's far from a sin!" K yelled.

Shanoai's eyes glowed the same as they had on Faerwai and a voice that was not her own crossed her lips. "Open the gate or she will rise from the seas, darkness personified, and call her children home."

"What the hell?" K looked at Shanoai, confused by the voice.

"Open the gate." The tall guard ordered, terror coloring her expression as she looked at Shanoai's glowing eyes.

"Again?" The sort guard scoffed. "You have got to be kidding me with this shit."

"Open the damn gate!" The two sang the key that allowed Shanoai and K to leave. "Don't come back here."

"No problem!" K promised as they were closed off from Sabrine and the mob of angry sirens.

NINE

"**Y**ou know we can't take the long way around this time, right?" Shanoai said as she got Liz ready for the next leg of their journey.

"You mean?" K perked up.

"The bridge." Shanoai nodded with a slight frown.

"Great. Maybe we'll get past it before the damn thing realizes we're there." The wolf remarked, but the excitement in her voice told that she was looking forward to action even if it meant facing a dragon.

"Let's keep that hope alive." Shanoai squinted. "You want us to fight that dragon, don't you?"

"I'm not saying I do, but I'm also not saying that I don't think it would be fun."

"Fun?" Shanoai laughed. "I'm rethinking having you along for this trip."

"You know you're loving my company." K undressed and

shifted into her wolf before Shanoai hopped on the back of Liz, who crop dusted the area as they took off.

They ran until they reached the edge of the lake and stopped just before the bridge. K shifted back to her human self so she could talk to Shanoai before they continued.

"Last chance to change your mind." The seer said.

"Why do I get the feeling this last chance moment isn't for me but for you?" K winked. "I'm good to go."

"Maybe it's for both of us." Shanoai looked out at the water that stirred with hidden movement.

"Look, standing here staring at the water will not make this happen any faster." K pointed to the bridge. "Besides, I'm naked and it's cold out here."

"Right, let's go." Shanoai readjusted atop Liz. "Run as fast as you can."

"Did you think I would take a leisurely stroll?" K returned to her wolf form and let out a low howl. She was ready to move ahead.

They made it to the middle of the bridge before they had any trouble. The water stirred beneath them, becoming more turbulent with each step that carried them forward on their path. Shanoai kept her eyes on the waters below them, so she was the first to see the beast emerge from within.

"Watch out!" Shanoai called out to K just as the dragon's foot hit the bridge.

K dodged the hit but stumbled, tumbling a few feet before she regained her footing. They kept running, dodging sharp teeth and claws. When they survived, the dragon changed its tactics, pummeling the bridge with shots of water that threatened to knock them over the side. If they fell into the water, there was no way they would survive.

The dragon shot out of the water, preparing for another blow that would surely destroy the bridge.

Liz reared back and screamed, knocking Shanoai off her back. Shanoai stood looking at the dragon, who had its sights on K.

Afraid that it would kill her new friend, she let out a bloody cry. "Stop!" Shanoai screamed and with the power of her voice came a beam of bright light that shot from her eyes.

The beam hit the dragon in the neck and burned its flesh. It screamed and returned to the water.

Shanoai caught up with Liz, jumped back on her back, and the three kept running. The dragon, clearly afraid of Shanoai's newfound power, didn't return for more.

"I take it you didn't know you could do that?" K asked after they reached the other side of the bridge. She'd shifted to her human form as she caught her breath.

"No, that's new." Shanoai jumped down from Liz's back. "I've never seen anything like that before, from a pixie or a seer."

"At least we know that song did its job." She wiped the sweat from her brow. "Dammit, that was close!"

"Yeah, it did." Shanoai looked worried. "Just wish I knew everything it changed."

"You'll have time to figure it out. Right now, we need to keep going. We have to stop a Cisk murder spree, remember?"

"Yeah, you're right. Let's keep moving."

It was another day of running for the wolf and the seer and their gassy horse. When the sunset again, they were standing outside of the great wall that stood erect around Moon Hollow. Though tired and sore, they had very little time to rest before Shanoai's vision came true.

"I can't believe I let you convince me to come here." K said as she pulled her shirt back over her head. "I can't stand witches, you know."

"I don't believe I convinced you to do anything." Shanoai pointed out. "You just wanted to get away from Sabrine."

"Yeah, well, I wasn't about to be caught dead there alone. Besides, you needed me." K boasted. "How could I turn my back on you at such a tragic time?"

"Look, I don't know why you are sticking by me, but thank you." Shanoai said honestly. "Tragic timing or not, I really appreciate our odd friendship."

"Well, it's stick with you or go back home. I don't think I have to repeat how I'm not looking forward to doing that." K pulled the bottle from her bag and drank the last of their water supply. "Meeting you came with the promise of adventure, and this has been a great one so far. Despite two near-death experiences."

"Glad you're enjoying it, but hopefully, it ends soon. I want to go home to see Charlie." Shanoai pulled the picture of her wife from her pocket. "I've never been away from her this long. Since we met, we've been together."

"Can't wait to let her know that you're fixed now?" K asked.

"Yes. For so long, she has been the only one who believed in me, you know? She stuck by my side and loved me when no one else would. It's going to be amazing, telling her it wasn't a waste of her time." Shanoai sighed and patted Liz on the side. The aerohorse was tired and rightfully so. She chewed on the berries Shanoai packed for her before leaving Sabrine.

"I doubt she would think it was a waste, even if you didn't have any special abilities. That's not how love works, and if it does, then it's not real."

"I just hope she is okay without me there." Shanoai put the picture back in her pocket. "Things aren't so great back home."

"I figured they weren't. Why else would you be here?" K looked at the sky where the last of the sunlight faded. "Are you sure you're on time? What if we missed them?"

"Well, this is where it happened," Shanoai pointed to a tall tree with red and purple leaves. "That tree was in the vision. They knocked down two of the branches in the fight. There's no damage yet, so I'm assuming we're on time."

"Good. We'll have time to rest up before they get here." K

yawned. "I need a nap. I should hunt, but sleep sounds like the better option right now."

"We need to hide Liz. If they get here and see her, they will know we're here." Shanoai looked around, trying to find a good place to stash the horse.

"You want the element of surprise?"

"Yes, I do." Shanoai said. "If they are coming here, it's under the direct order of someone powerful. The Cisks don't act without direction."

"Corruption in Mosail?" K perked up. "Never thought I'd see the day."

"Yes, it appears so." Shanoai shook her head. "The sad part about it is that you never think it will happen to your people. You know? You hear about corruption and evil taking over other territories, but you always think your home is safe from it. Nowhere is safe."

"You're damn right." K muttered.

Tucked away in the shadows, they waited for the Cisks to arrive. They talked again about life, dreams, and what they wanted for themselves. Shanoai wanted to spend her life with Charlie. She wanted to have a family and finally feel like a whole person. All K wanted was the freedom to choose her own path in life.

"Why can't you choose?" Shanoai asked. "I know I said I wouldn't pry, but I'd honestly like to know. What stops you from deciding?"

"I guess I can tell you the truth now, after all we've been through." K took a deep breath.

"I'm all ears." Shanoai waited.

"My father is the Alpha of The Den." K said with a smirk. "That's why. I'm the daughter of the alpha and he runs my life."

"Wait, *the* alpha? You mean the head alpha?" Shanoai asked. The Den's governance comprised five packs, each having its own leader. Over them all, was the one Alpha. Their structure was very similar to Mosail.

"Yes, and as his daughter, it is imperative that I be the picture of perfection." K nodded with the tight smile. "I'm sure you already can tell that I don't measure up to what my father would prefer."

"I've been running around Novia with the head alpha's daughter." Shanoai shook her head. "And here I was thinking I put your life at risk."

"He has scouts all over. No doubt reporting back where I've been, even if they don't know why I've gone on this journey. I will go back eventually." Her friend sighed, defeated. "I have to. Even if all I want to do is hop on a boat and sail to the other side of the world."

"So that's why you can't just take a trip when you want, well, not before this." Shanoai asked, still wondering why this instance was any different for K. What made it worth the risk for her?

"Being the Alpha's daughter comes with a lot of responsibilities, ones that I don't always know that I want." K answered honestly.

115

"Still, I couldn't leave. There was this sense of fear that if I left, it would mean horrible things for my family. I couldn't live with that. But I don't know. I met you and that changed. You–" K stopped when she looked up at Shanoai.

Shanoai's eyes glowed with the light of the moon as she looked at her friend. She received her second vision. An image of K standing between two paths. One that led toward her home and the other into the unknown. Soon, she would no longer be able to run from the decisions she avoided making.

"What was that?" K asked. "Are you okay?"

"Yeah, I'm fine. It was a vision." Shanoai rubbed her forehead. "I need to get used to those."

"What did you see?" K leaned closer to Shanoai. "Shan, what did you see?"

"I saw you, standing between two paths." She answered. "One that lead to The Den and the other away from it."

"What does that mean?"

"Soon you're going to have to decide. I'm assuming it's one that you've avoided making for a while. You won't be able to dodge it for much longer."

"Oh, that's ominous." K nodded. "I guess I'll deal with that when I get there." She sniffed the air. "We got action."

One by one the Cisks appeared as their aerohorses came to a stop just outside the border of Moon Hollow. They waited to see what would happen.

"If they find us here–" K started.

"They won't." Shanoai said confidently. "They don't know there's a reason to be concerned. It's one of their downfalls. They rely too much on the visions of their leaders."

"Someone's coming." K sniffed the air.

"Who?" Shanoai scanned the area but saw no one.

"You won't believe it if I told you." She pointed to the wall, where there was a ripple in the darkness.

Two men stepped from the shadows. One thin but strong with the ability to cross shadows. The other muscular with long dreadlocks that hung down his back in a collected braid and a leather jacket with a familiar symbol on the shoulder.

"The shadow walker and the peacekeeper. Same two that were in the woods outside The Den." K said.

"And so, our paths cross." Shanoai nodded as she watched one of the Cisks drop from their horse and approached the two men. "What are they saying?"

"The Cisk is asking about some relic or something." K listened in. "Whatever it is, they want the shadow walker to hand it over."

"You think he will?" Shanoai asked and her answer came a moment later when the shadow walker punched the Cisks in the face.

"I think that's a no." K chuckled. "I never would have thought him the type to knock out a Cisk."

Despite the shadow walker's bravado, the Cisks were unphased. They knew what they were dealing with before they came. A net made of meranium dropped over the shadow walker; a technique they often used to make sure that shadow walkers couldn't get away.

With the shadow walker trapped and the peacekeeper quickly surrounded, Shanoai knew she had to act. It wouldn't be long before the Cisks got whatever it was they came for and her instincts told her she had to help stop that from happening.

"Wait here." She told K. "I don't want them to know you're on my side if they don't need to."

"Element of surprise." K nodded, but still stripped away her clothing. She'd be ready if Shanoai needed her.

Shanoai ran to join the battle. She'd catch hell at some point for fighting her own, but she had to trust her gut. Her instincts told her to protect the shadow walker at all costs. Unsure of how to control her new powers, she fought the way she was trained. With her fists and her blades. Her arrival was a surprise to the Cisk. She knocked out three before they realized she was there.

She wanted to avoid using lethal force but the fourth put up more of a fight. When she realized it was her life or theirs, she could make only one decision. She lifted the blade and slid it across their throat. After they fell she went to work setting their horse free, but she was spotted.

Still, she ran through the field with precision. Of the fifteen Cisks, Shanoai knocked out seven before she made it to the center of their attack. The peacekeeper hard at work fighting off the others. She knelt down and released the shadow walker. When he was free, the three stood back to back, sizing up their opponents. Another wave of Cisks were coming.

"Who are you?" The peacekeeper asked.

"Think we can do the introduction part later? I'm on your side." Shanoai said. "For now, that's all you need to know."

"Good enough for me." The shadow walker nodded and stepped into the shadows.

Twenty more Cisks arrived on the field outside of Moon Hollow. Shanoai expected the witch guards to show up and do something, but they did not.

"The High Priestess doesn't care about an attack outside her city?" She asked.

"Beats me," the peacekeeper said just before punching another Cisk in the jaw.

"I guess Mosail isn't the only place with its problems right now."

"No, it isn't." He grunted.

The three fought as hard as they could. Even with the shadow walker using the darkness to his advantage, the Cisks still outnumbered them. Shanoai thought about her friend moments before the wolf appeared. The large gray body appeared in a flash of fur and teeth. Her appearance took the Cisks by surprised and that alone gave them the advantage they needed.

Shanoai still held back her powers. Instincts screamed that this was not the time to show them off.

What worked was K's howl. She dropped her head back and let her call reach into the sky. In the surrounding shadows, eyes glowed. Moments later, a symphony of growls vibrated the air. She was right when she said her father's people were following them.

The wolves didn't need to do anything more. The Cisks, afraid of being ripped apart by the unexpected addition to the fight, ran. They all tried to get away, but Shanoai held one behind after slicing open their left leg.

"Who are you working for?" Shanoai asks the Cisks questions, but they refused to answer.

"Fine, you don't want to cooperate, I'll make this work for myself." Shanoai's eyes glowed as she found the answer within herself. The key to getting what she needed.

She sat on the Cisk's chest, pinning them to the ground. When they could no longer move, she ripped the protective helmet from their head and forced them to look into her eyes.

"This is going to hurt." She said before digging her thumbs into their eyes.

"Dammit, that's gross." K said as she returned to her human form.

"Um…" The peacekeeper cleared his throat, then handed the wolf his jacket.

"Oh, thanks." K accepted his offer.

The three watched Shanoai as she focused those glowing eyes on the Cisk beneath her. A few moments later, she let go and her eyes returned to normal.

"I know who it is." She announced, standing over the now unconscious Cisk.

"Who is it?" K asked.

"Someone very powerful." Shanoai answered.

"I hate to interrupt, but we need to get moving." The peacekeeper said.

"We can't let them get back to Mosail." Shanoai said. "They will tell what happened here."

"I'll handle it." The shadow walker grabbed the Cisk and vanished.

"K?" Shanoai turned to the wolf.

"Yes." K answered. "What's up, Shan?"

"You up for more adventure or you ready to go home?"

K looked over her shoulder to the line of trees where the wolves waited. "Always ready for more. What do you need?"

"I need you to take Liz back to Mosail. Find Charlie." Shanoai explained. "Tell her that Mauor is behind this. She needs to tell Waoli. The Sukra are not on her side. I also need you to let her know I'm okay. Tell her that what we planned, it worked out. Better than we could have imagined. I'm whole again and so is she."

"Um, okay. Is she supposed to know what that means?"

"Yes, she will."

K nodded.

"What about you?" She asked. "You not coming with me?"

"I need to go with them." Shanoai answered. "My path doesn't lead home. Not yet."

"Another one of those gut instincts?" K asked as she removed the jacket from her shoulders and tossed it back to its owner.

"Yes." Shanoai nodded. "Do you trust me?"

"Oddly, I do." The she-wolf turned to walk away, then stopped. "Be careful, Shan. Remember, we're supposed to have a vacation on the beach. You owe me a drink when we get there."

"I'll see you there." Shanoai watched as K retrieved Liz from her hiding spot, redressed, and headed toward Mosail.

"You're coming with us?" The peacekeeper asked.

"Yes, I have to." Shanoai answered. "You're going to need me. I don't know why or for what, but you will."

After Liz and K disappeared, the shadow walker returned.

"Is now a good time for introductions?" He asked.

"Shanoai." She held her hand out.

"I'm Maze." The shadow walker shook her hand, then pointed to the peacekeeper. "This is Shaw."

"Nice to meet you both." Shanoai turned to look at the sky when the sound of a dragon's cry rang out in the distance. "I think we have something to take care of."

The Peackeeper's Promise

ONE

They rode the shadows from Dragonia all the way back to the frozen mountain ranges where The Last Keep stood. In the coldest place in Novia, the peacekeepers were safe from intruders. Stepping out of the darkness, Maze looked up at the fortress and huffed.

"Woah." Maze looked up at the tall stone wall that shut out the rest of the world. "This has to be one of the last places I ever thought I would see in person."

"Not exactly a chosen stop on the tourist guides." Shaw shook off the weird feeling walking through shadows left him with.

"Have you figured out what you're going to tell them about me yet?" Maze shuddered from the extreme drop in temperature and rubbed his hands over his arms, trying to warm up. "I know they aren't expecting you to return home with a guest."

"They know about you. I told them I would recruit the help of a shadow walker." Shaw scratched his chin. "But you're right, they won't be expecting me to bring you back here. Your presence alone will alert the others that something is wrong."

"A guest automatically means something is wrong?" Maze rubbed his hands together and blew on them for warmth. "I mean, do you guys ever bring anyone back here who isn't already a Peacekeeper?"

"Not anyone we expect to go free again." Shaw teased with a crooked smile.

"Should I step my ass back into the shadows?" Maze pointed over his shoulder at the retreating darkness. "Is it too late for me to change my mind about this?"

"You're safe here." Shaw reassured him with a chuckle. "It's unusual, but I will vouch for you. As long as I do, they won't touch you. I'll make sure of that."

"That's comforting." He looked at the wall. It was brick solid and stood around the entire border of their territory. "So, how do we get in? Are we meant to climb up there? I've seen a lot of border walls, all magically delicious, but typically you can tell where the entrance is. I can't even see the top of this damn thing."

"Nothing that dramatic. There is a doorway, it's just hidden really well. They'll open the gates after I signal them to do so." Shaw gave Maze a serious look. "All jokes aside, this is your last chance to turn back, Maze."

"Do what you need to do so we can get out of this cold please." Maze brushed off the offer. "I'd like to not freeze my balls off out here."

Shaw reached into the front pocket of his jacket and took out a small white whistle. He placed the tool between his lips and blew on it, but it made no sound. A few moments later, the snow shifted on the barrier wall and the center of the wall split open to reveal a small path that led into the city.

"How did you do that?" Maze looked confused.

"There is a receiver in the tower."

"This reminds me of all of those anime movies that the Zanissa's dad used to bring back from Earth. This would be one of those ominous moments where the two heroes are walking into a trap." Maze put his hand on Shaw's shoulder, stopping him from continuing. "Wait, you don't think this could be a trap, right?"

"I think you need to ease off the anime. This is my home. These are my people. This is not a trap." Shaw put his hand on Maze's back, pushing him forward. "And this gate doesn't stay open for long, so unless you want to get crushed in between stone, I suggest we keep moving."

Maze allowed Shaw to usher him through the stone entrance. The path was one hundred feet long. When they made it to the other side, the walls slid shut again, sealing them off from the outside world. Inside, the world was different. Shaw watched with a slight smile as Maze took in the bustling community.

"This is medieval." Maze remarked as he took in the stone towers and thickly dressed attire of the people moving around.

"Not a lot of advancement in the icy tundra." Shaw said. "It's not that bad though. We do have technology. You just have to look closely to see it." He pointed to the wires above their head. "For instance, those wires are part of a larger circuit that provide power for the entire city. Also, for the armory."

"Of course, you would have advanced weapons tech. Explains the shooting light blades." Maze pointed to Shaw's side where the empty hilt hung.

"And that's just the beginning." Shaw said proudly. "Maybe one day I'll show you."

"Shaw, you're back. That took longer than we thought it would." Rosalee, a snow leopard with bright eyes and a tough outer layer, was the first to welcome him home. Hooded and covered from the elements, only her face was visible to them. She spoke with a soft drawl that softened the intimidation she always tried to give off. "You decide to turn the trip into a vacation? I know you've been feeling cooped up here…"

"A vacation would have been the preference, but no." Shaw shook hands with the woman. "Unfortunately, we ran into some complications."

"What complications?" Rosalee asked, glancing at Maze with a raised brow. "The kind that calls for visitors, I see. Unheard of."

"The kind that I need to report in before I talk to anyone else. Is Silas here?" He asked, ignoring her questioning gaze.

"That bad, huh?" She turned and looked up at the tower that stood tallest over the Keep. "Your timing in impeccable. Silas just got back here not too long ago."

"What kind of mood is he in?" He followed her line of sight.

"I didn't talk to him, but he didn't look happy. Apparently, he found a few problems of his own on his trip." She shrugged. "You know it's best to stay out of his way when that happens."

"That's not good." Shaw considered his options. "I don't have a choice. I have to talk to him because we have some serious trouble heading our way."

"Trouble?" She lowered her voice. Shaw wasn't the type to be worried unless there was really something to worry about. "What kind of trouble?"

"The kind that breathes fire." He looked her in the eye and witnessed the fear, short-lived as it may have been.

"You mean the dragons?" Rosalee pulled him to the side away from the flow of traffic and raised a brow when the stranger he hadn't yet introduced followed them. "They're active again? Are you sure?"

"You know how this works, Rosalee. I have to talk to Silas before anyone else." Shaw shook his head. It was protocol. Give the big guy all details and he decided what the rest needed to know.

"And what is he doing here?" She pointed to Maze. "I don't recall your agenda saying anything about bringing back a shadow walker. Are you recruiting new peacekeepers in your spare time?"

"He saved my life. He stays with me." Shaw asserted. "And no, he isn't becoming a peacekeeper."

"So, you're just bringing home strays now?" She prodded

further, wanting whatever information she could get about his guest.

"Save it, Rosalee." Shaw warned.

"Hey, you know I love to pick at you." She laughed. "Find me after your chat with Silas. You still owe me a drink."

Rosalee walked away. She waved at another Peacekeeper as she did, looking over her shoulder at Maze as she left them. She had a walk that would draw you in and hidden beneath the heavy coat, muscles that would knock you right back out.

"I take it you two are lifelong friends?" Maze asked as Shaw continued walking and he followed.

"Something like that." Shaw headed for the tower where Rosalee indicated Silas was. "Come on, we need to get this over with."

"Was she born into this like you?" Maze asked as he followed.

"No, but she came into it earlier than most." Shaw answered honestly. "Rosalee and I grew up together. Annoying as she is, she's like a sister to me. A little sister who always bugs me to buy her drinks she can definitely afford to pay for herself."

"Is your sister going to kill me? I kind of got the feeling she might try to end my life." Maze stuck close to Shaw. "Almost like she would enjoy it."

"No," Shaw chuckled. "She's just trying to get a feel for you. Make sure you won't try to hurt anyone while you're here or you're not secretly here trying to spy."

"Does anyone ever come here to try to spy on you?" Maze looked around. "How exactly would that work?"

"You'd be surprised. Not everyone in the world is afraid of a Peacekeeper. There are also a lot of valuable things inside these walls. Some of those things people think are worth dying for."

"Well, let your friends here know that I'm not one of those people." Maze nearly tripped over himself as he watched a giant man walking by carrying what he hoped was an animal carcass on his shoulder. "I don't think anything is more valuable than my own life."

"Oh, they know. You wouldn't be inside these walls if they didn't trust my judgement. If you were an enemy, you'd already be dead."

"I guess that's somewhat comforting."

They stopped outside of the doors to the tower. He turned to speak to Maze who he realized was shivering. Shaw took off his coat and handed it to the man, who quickly put it on.

"Better?" He asked.

"Yes, thank you. I'm not used to these temperatures."

"Good. Okay. When we go in here, let me do all the talking. Only speak if Silas talks to you, no one else." Shaw instructed. "Got it?"

"Only talk to the head guy. Understood." Maze mimed zipping his lips closed.

"Silas isn't the friendliest. Don't take it personally if he doesn't address you at all." Shaw continued. "It wouldn't be the first time he's done it."

"I'm used to it, trust me." Maze nodded. "Can we please go inside now?"

Shaw turned and opened the heavy door, pushing it aside to reveal the dark interior. They walked into a room with four benches and an extensive set of winding stairs to the highest point. Silas' home allowed him to see all vantage points. If anything dared to come there, any threat at all, he would see it.

"We're walking up there?" Maze blanched. "Right, no elevator here."

"There is one, but it's not for public use." Shaw winked.

"Dammit." Maze shook his head and followed Shaw, who'd already headed up the steps. "I just gotta say, this seems like a horrible inefficient use of your time."

"Suck it up." Shaw looked back at Maze, already falling behind. "Pick up the pace."

Maze muttered something beneath his breath, but Shaw couldn't hear what he said. As they climbed the stairs, they passed several doors, all closed. Maze started to question the doors, but they heard footsteps descending the steps above them.

Moments later, they passed two men who smelled of grass and spring rains. An unusual smell in the ice-covered mountains. Shaw noted their clothes and the dirt on their hands and skin. Something wasn't right. Rosalee said that Silas found trouble. It had to have something to do with the unfamiliar men.

"Stay here," Shaw instructed as they reached the top of the steps that opened to another room with three benches and a tall brown door. "I need to talk to him before we bring you into this conversation."

"Is it safe for me here?" Maze looked uncomfortable. There were no other people in the room, but he still appeared worried.

"You're fine. Just have a seat and I'll come get you when we're ready for you."

Shaw knocked on the door and waited until he was told to come in. When he got the affirmation, he looked at Maze once more, then entered the room, leaving the shadow walker alone.

"Shaw, it's good to see you have returned safely." Silas welcomed him with his baritone voice. The bear shifter was large in both size and personality. He wore a pair of black wire glasses that sat on the tip of his wide nose beneath the head of short gray hair.

Silas was the Peacekeeper General. He oversaw all the activity of the protectors of Novia. There used to be more in his position, when there were other Keeps. Now, he was the last and the weight of their responsibility in the world fell on his shoulders.

"It's good to be home." Shaw responded. "Sorry it took so

long."

"It took as long as it needed to take." Silas said. "Were you careful, safe?"

"Yes, always." Shaw confirmed.

"Then that is all that matters." Silas headed for the bar next to the window and poured himself a glass of whiskey. "What did you find on your trip?"

"Nothing you're going to be happy about." Shaw said, happy the bear already had a drink in hand. The smell of the dark liquor was enticing even to him.

"So bad news, let me top off my drink before you continue. I've had just about all the bad news I can take." Silas knocked back the drink, refilled the glass, then sat down behind the massive desk. "Bring it on."

"The disturbance in the Tendrils was real. The threat not quite what we expected, but I've taken care of it, for now." Shaw said, leaving out details of the vampires. He wanted Silas focused on the important part, the dragons.

"Well, that to me sounds like good news, Shaw." Silas tapped on the desk. "What aren't you telling me?"

"You're right. There's more." Shaw nodded and stepped closer to the desk.

"Of course not. What else is there?"

"As we were leaving, there was an explosion." Shaw continued his report.

"An explosion?" The bear perked up. "I don't have any other reports of an explosion."

"Well, there was one. In Dragonia. It shook the ground for miles around us."

"Did you go check it out?"

"Yes, thanks to the shadow walker." Shaw nodded. "We were able to get closer than I think we've ever been."

"You actually got a shadow walker to help you?" Silas laughed. "Dammit, you're good. I just knew your plan to make that happen would never work out. Galari just handed one over to you?"

"Yes, with some convincing. They had him locked up, his family in debt, so he was ready to make a deal." Shaw explained. "He was also in deep shit with the High Priestess, so she was open to sending him off to his potential death."

"So, this shadow walker took you to Dragonia, where you saw what?" Silas refocused the conversation.

"We saw her, the queen." Shaw cut to the point. "Last thing I ever thought we'd find, but she was there. Alive, no longer sleeping."

"Are you sure about this?" Silas asked as he straightened in his seat. "Shaw, this isn't something you can make a mistake about."

"I'm sure. Silas, we stood in the shadows and watched it happen." Shaw took a deep breath as he recalled what he witnessed. "She stepped out of this massive jade egg, where I assume she's been sleeping all this time. Killed one of her own people just moments after she woke up. She's back, and she is pissed off and I don't know how much longer we have before she retaliates."

"Where is the shadow walker? Is that him I smell outside the door?" Silas pointed to the closed door behind Shaw.

"Yes." Shaw looked over his shoulder. "He insisted on coming back with me."

"Well, bring him in, so we can get his account of events." Silas knocked back the rest of his drink. "Fuck."

Shaw nodded and left the room to get Maze. He found the man pacing outside the door.

"Finally," Maze said. "Is everything okay?"

"He wants to speak with you." Shaw looked back at the door where their leader waited.

"Me? Really?" He looked shocked. "I really thought you two would speak, and we'd leave. You know, without me being interrogated again."

"Yes, just stay calm. Silas is a bear shifter." Shaw warned. "Answer his questions honestly and there will be no issues."

"Right. Okay." Maze agreed, and Shaw opened the door.

The two entered the room to find Silas standing by the bar refilling his drink.

"You're the shadow walker brave enough to enter the Tendrils with a peacekeeper?" Silas asked as he put the whiskey back on the bar.

"Yes, that's me." Maze smiled awkwardly.

"What's your name?" Silas asked.

"Maze."

"Big balls for shadow walker. You know, I used to know one of your kind." Silas took a deep breath. "He was a tall guy and had big red hair. Also brave as fuck, name was Baskiet."

"Thomas Baskiet?" Maze asked with wide eyes.

"Yes, you know him?"

"He..." Maze paused. "He was my grandfather."

"I see where you get your balls from now." The bear laughed. "Baskiet was a beast like no other. He did things I didn't know shadow walkers were capable of. But I'm sure you know all about him."

"I don't know as much as I would like to." Maze answered honestly.

"Tell me what you saw, Maze." Silas returned to his desk. "What happened on your journey with our Shaw?"

"You mean the demon vampire or the rebirth of the dragon queen."

"Demon vampire?" Silas looked at Shaw who'd clearly left out details from his report.

"That is the original threat we saw." Shaw jumped in.

"The one that is under control now?" Silas raised a brow. "Why didn't you mention this before?"

"I didn't mention it because its handled, for the time being. We will need to look into it further I'm sure, but right now the dragon is the major concern."

"I'll take your word on that." Silas nodded. "So, the Dragon Queen is reborn."

"Yes, and immediately after she stepped out of that egg, she killed one guy and sent out four scouts." Maze said. "That woman is terrifyingly powerful."

"How did this happen?" Silas asked.

"I think it's connected to the Tendrils." Shaw answered. "I can't explain it, but the energy there was dark, and it broke through into the waters."

"The waters surrounding Dragonia." Silas looked at the map of Novia that hung on the wall left of his desk.

"Yes, the dark energy, the explosion, it's all connected somehow." Shaw pointed out. "None of this is a coincidence. It feels too strategic to be happenstance."

"We need to handle this, but there is something else we have to deal with." Silas said, then looked at Maze. "This doesn't concern you. I'm thankful for your help and we welcome here you as long as it's necessary, but you understand I must talk to Shaw alone now."

"I'll wait outside." Maze stepped back out of the room into the hall.

"What's going on?" Shaw asked Silas after the door closed, leaving the two alone in his office.

"We have identified another threat coming from the north." Silas responded as he rolled up the sleeves of his gray shirt to reveal arms covered in tattoos. "Perfect timing for the shit to start piling up."

"The north?" Shaw thought about what he said. "What threat comes from the north?"

"Trolls." Silas said incredulously. "Of all things, trolls."

"Trolls? Since when are trolls a threat to us?" Shaw couldn't believe what he was hearing. If anything, he would have thought it the wolves or the bears, but trolls were typically gentle creatures who never had any run-ins with peacekeepers.

"Since they've become organized. There are others working with them." Silas rubbed his forehead. "I can't figure out who it is, but someone is rallying the trolls. And their strength of numbers alone is something to be concerned about. They've already expanded their borders."

"You think it's a power play?" The peacekeeper considered the information he heard. Someone wanted to use the trolls as tools. It made sense, but who could be behind it?

"Yes, I think that's exactly what this is. We just need to figure out who would think to use the trolls as muscle for their own gains. We haven't dug that part up, but we're close."

"The two in the hall, covered in dirt, smelling like a field of wild grass. Are they in on this?" Shaw spoke of the two strangers he passed on the steps. "I don't recognize them."

"Yes, astute as always." Silas said. "You know we have sleepers all over Novia. Their base is near the troll territory. They've reported heightened activity. Not sure it's safe to be out there anymore."

"What do you need from me?" Shaw asked, ready to do whatever Silas needed from him.

"I need you to figure out this dragon thing. You were there, you saw what was going on." Silas looked out the window to scan the sky. "You know what to do. Scout it out and confirm what's going on here."

"What do you think it means? Her waking after all this time?" Shaw joined him by the window. They were a long way from the dragon's territory, but the concern that their winged enemies would arrive and light up the sky was there.

"I think it means all those bad omens they warned us of are coming to head. There are so many changes happening in Novia now. That is no coincidence." Silas said. "I only wish I knew where all this was headed."

"She is going to want her egg." Shaw said the thing he'd been avoiding saying aloud.

"I thought of that. An egg that we don't even know still exists."

"There was rumor." Shaw said. "But even if it was true, she's been sleeping for over a century. What are the odds it's still around or even viable?"

"Yes, I know of the rumor. Your job now it to find out if it was true. I hate to say this, because you just got back, but you will not be hanging around the Keep for very long."

"Long enough to get Rosalee that drink." Shaw smirked.

"Yeah, and after you do, send her my way. I want her in this troll situation." Silas said. "I planned for it to be both of you, but I think she can handle this without you. I'll let her choose a team."

"Things are really bad, aren't they?" Shaw looked at the bar where the whiskey sat.

"Yes, they are." Silas followed his line of sight and walked over to the bar. He poured himself another drink and offered one to Shaw who accepted the offer. "And they're going to get a lot worse. But we've seen bad before."

"We've seen bad, but not this much and not all at once." Shaw sipped his drink. "I just wish I knew what the hell was going on in our world."

"As long as we stay on top of things, we'll be fine." Silas reassured. "Enjoy your night at home. Show your new friend a good time before the two of you head off to chase the dragons."

"You think he is going to go that far with me?" The peacekeeper asked. "I don't know how long he'll be up for risking his life."

"Hell, he came to the Keep. I know you, Shaw." Silas raised his brow. "You didn't invite him to come here."

"No, I didn't." Shaw nodded. "He offered. I would never ask anyone to come here."

"Exactly." Silas returned to his desk. "Well, if you ask me, I think that means you have a partner now."

"I don't do partners." Shaw's jaw tightened as the sun lowered in the sky casting its orange light on his dark skin. He squinted in the light.

"No, you don't. I know that." Silas said. "Shaw, what happened to Hank was bad. But it wasn't your fault."

"Silas, I–" Shaw started, but Silas held up his hand to stop him.

"I know. You don't want to talk about it. I respect that. Just saying, don't cut yourself off from the possibilities. We may be close to the end of the world. You don't want to miss any opportunities now."

"Are there any opportunities that you might be missing out on?" Shaw tried to turn the conversation from his personal life and avoid the pain in his chest he still felt when he thought about his former partner.

144

"Yes, I'm sure there are, they just aren't as obvious." Silas got back up and ushered Shaw to the door. "Now, get some rest, have a few drinks for me, and let me know your plan tomorrow. This doesn't feel like something we can wait on."

"Will do." He shook Silas' hand.

"I mean it, Shaw." Silas held his hand in his as he spoke. "Don't choose to stay blind to what's right in front of you."

TWO

"How did it go?" Maze asked Shaw as he exited Silas' office. This time, he was sitting on one of the wooden benches, a pensive look on his face.

"It went well." Shaw looked back at the door. "Better than I thought it would go, honestly."

"Is that a good thing?" Maze followed him, who headed for the stairs.

"I'm not sure." He responded. "It appears there are a lot more going on than just the dragons."

"There is?" Maze questioned. "Like what? Anything we need to be worried about?"

"Yes, but we're staying focused on this." Shaw looked back at Maze. "Dragons are bigger than any other threat for us right now."

"So, what are we going to do?"

Shaw stopped, turned and stepped back up to look Maze in the eye. "You really are hanging around, aren't you? Despite

147

everything."

"I told you, this is my fate as much as it is yours." Maze said without hesitation. "We're in this together, Shaw. Get over it."

"Alright, well, we'll be moving on soon. But we'll spend the night here." Shaw continued down the steps. Halfway down, he noticed one of the doors that was usually closed, stood partially open, but as they approached it, the door slammed shut. Whoever was inside didn't want to be known.

"A night among Peacekeepers. How fun!" Maze said, seemingly oblivious.

"I'm sure you're in for a thrill ride." Shaw chuckled as they exited the tower and Maze pulled the borrowed coat tighter around his body. "My home isn't too far from here. We'll stop there first, rest up, and get you something warmer to wear."

"Lead the way. I hope you have working heat in your place."

"Of course, I do. Or at least I did before I left." Shaw teased.

He lived in what they called the Stacks. Basically, apartments for Peacekeepers. Those who were rarely home and lived minimal lives while they were there. Others lived in the Stacks, because of convenience. They were close to the markets and to the local bars and restaurants.

Shaw's home was an adequate reflection of him. He had very little furniture, a closet full of weapons, and an empty fridge. He did, however, have a giant bed with plush bedding. Sleep was important. When he was away from home, he often slept in tents atop rough grounds. Home had to be better than that.

"Make yourself at home," Shaw said as they entered the apartment. He turned the lights on and immediately adjusted the heat. "It usually warms up pretty quickly."

"I hope so." Maze's teeth chattered.

"After it does, you can take a shower and I'll give you fresh clothes to wear. I'm stockier than you, but I think you'll be fine."

"More room for layers." Maze said. "I seriously don't understand how you live here."

"Conditioning." Shaw said as he grabbed a glass bottle of water from the fridge.

"You have refrigerators, central heat, and yet no elevators." Maze rolled his eyes. "I mean, you live on the fifth floor!"

"Walking is good. It keeps up stamina." Shaw pointed to the closed door that led out of his home. "Stairs keep your lungs strong. You need that here when it really gets cold."

"It gets colder than this?"

"This is nothing." He winked. The vent above his head opened and warm air flowed into the room. "Ah, there it is. Only a few minutes now for warmth."

As promised, when the apartment warmed, Maze took a

shower and redressed in Peacekeeper standards. The thermals, though a bit baggy on him, kept him warm while he rested. Shaw freshened up himself and changed his clothes while Maze slept on the single sofa in the front room. There wasn't much to his single bedroom home, but he liked it.

Once dressed, he woke Maze from his nap so they could leave in search of food. There were plenty of options in The Last Keep, despite the climate. Whenever Shaw was home, he would restock his fridge with drinks and short items and eat most of his meals at a pub not far from his home.

"Food here isn't what you can get in Moon Hollow, but it's decent." Shaw cautioned as they entered Avo, the bar named after its owner's pet dog.

"I'm not expecting the best cuisine of Novia. Everyone knows you go to Kilosh for that." Maze joked. "I just need fuel for the tank."

"And take your chances with those songbirds? Good luck with that." Shaw said. "There's a lot I will do for a good meal, but that's not on the list."

"You know, I heard it's because of their water." Maze shook his finger in Shaw's face.

"What?" He frowned and slapped his finger away as the smell of beer and brisket filled his head. His stomach growled with forgotten hunger.

"Their food is so good because they only cook using the water from the Lynk pond." Maze kept close to Shaw walking through the establishment. "Anything they ingest is prepared with that water. Supposed to keep their voices prime."

"That would make sense. I mean, it has magical properties that I don't think even the birds understand." Shaw waved to a table full of his friends, then headed in the opposite direction. He wouldn't subject Maze to their banter, or have them digging for information he couldn't provide.

"You say that like you want a chance to figure it out." Maze said, narrowly missing a waitress carrying a tray of beers. "Sorry!" He apologized for nearly knocking her over.

"Hey, I'm a peacekeeper. A big part of the job is trying to understand the unknown." Shaw shrugged.

"Well, I'm on the side of some things staying unknown." Maze rubbed his stomach. "What I'd like to get to know now is some food. Preferably meat, packed with protein. All that shadow walking really takes it out of me."

"Sit." Shaw pointed to a table in the corner. "I'll get us something to eat and drink and put in an order for food."

"Excellent." Maze clapped his hands and made a beeline for the table tucked away from the general population.

"Shaw, good to see you're back." The bartender, a stocky woman name Ral, greeted him. "Oh, and you've brought home a pet this time."

"Chill, Ral." Shaw warned. "He's a friend, and he's helping me on my case."

"Right, that makes sense." She glanced at the table where Maze sat. "Doesn't hurt that he's a cutie either."

"Beer, two mugs and a pitcher." He avoided her comment. Just as he suspected, everyone was ready to pry.

As Ral prepared his order, he turned, leaning his back against the bar and scanned the room. His friends watched him closely, glancing between him and the table where Maze sat. Everyone had questions, but most people knew better to keep them to themselves.

Shaw had a reputation of being something of a hothead. It got worse after losing his partner. Counseling helped, but there were still moments when he felt like he could lose himself. It took more effort than he liked to remain level-headed. And it was worse when he was home with all the people who reminded him constantly of what he lost.

"Here you go, big shot." Ral pulled him from his thoughts, and he turned to find the tray with the requested items. "You getting food, too? Or are you on a liquid diet?"

"Two Peacekeeper platters." Shaw ordered the standard meal that consisted of whale steaks and potatoes. Potatoes weren't natural to Novia. Like other plants, someone had transported them from Earth. The peacekeepers took to them and started including them in most meals.

"Got two ready now if you want them." Ral pulled the plates from the order window. "Standing order for Masto, but he's not back from diving yet."

"Great, I'll take them. Thanks."

152

Ral added the plates to Shaw's tray and waved him off. "Get before someone sees you and tells me I'm playing favorites again."

"You're the best, Ral." He left the bar and headed to Maze, who looked at him with a cheerful expression. For a moment, he wondered how long they would have together and if a day would come when he didn't get to see that look on his face again.

"This looks amazing." Maze said with wide eyes after Shaw put the tray on the table.

"You must be starving if this bar food looks amazing to you." Shaw laughed and handed Maze a beer.

"We've been living off a steady diet of berries and water for a few days. So yeah, this looks like a feast fit for a king."

"Well, your highness, eat up." Shaw sat down in the chair next to Maze.

"So what's next? We chase after the dragons?" Maze asked as he started cutting into the steak.

"Something like that." Shaw took a sip from his drink. "We need to find what she wants before we face her."

"Find what the Dragon Queen wants?" Maze popped the piece of meat in his mouth. "I take it you have an idea about what that is?"

"Yeah, I do." Shaw nodded and salted his potatoes. "Something that was taken from her. It's the reason the war between the dragons and the Peacekeepers happened."

"You took something from her?" Maze stopped chewing, wide eyes staring at Shaw. "How? Why?"

"Well, not me, but someone did." Shaw clarified. "I wasn't even born when it happened."

"Right, so someone stole something. The war happened. Then they put the queen in a magical coma." Maze recounted. "What did they take?"

"Yes. And what they took was–"

"Shaw!" Rosalee called out as she danced across the bar, already clearly inebriated. "You here to buy my next drink?"

No longer covered in her coat and hood, Rosalee showed off her form as she moved across the floor. She wore a pair of fitted jeans and a loose button up top that hung from her shoulders. Her wild hair fell free around her muscled shoulders and her face was flush with heat.

"It looks like you've already had plenty, Rosa." Shaw muttered. "I think you're good for the night."

"Never, I can always use more." She sat down and looked at Maze. "Not sure we ever met officially. I'm Rosalee."

"Nice to meet you, Rosalee. I'm Maze." He shook her hand in between bites.

"Maze, are you enjoying our frosty home?" She leaned across the table.

"Better now that Shaw has loaned me some of his clothes, though they are a little big on me." Maze lifted his arm to show the loose fabric. "Still better than what I had before."

"Luckily he is such a caring guy." Rosalee winked at Shaw.

"What else would you expect from me?" He asked, finally enjoying his own meal.

"Nothing less." Rosalee leaned back in her chair. "Despite you not buying me a drink. So how was your trip? You're free to give me details now I take it."

"Yes, I am." Shaw nodded. "It was one of my most interesting ones I've had."

"Do tell." She said as she eyed the pitcher of beer.

"How does one explain a trip that takes you into the city of witches, through the wolves' den, and a quick visit with the Pixie Queen before heading into a forest infested with demonic spirits?"

"Damn, and that's just the recap?" She laughed. "And what did all that get you?"

"A demonic vampire and the awakening of the Dragon Queen."

Rosalee coughed, then lowered her voice so no one else could hear her. "The Dragon Queen? You can't be serious."

"I wish I wasn't." Shaw chugged his beer. "But I saw her with my own eyes."

155

She looked over her shoulder. The bar was quiet. Few people came before the sun went down. "Are you going to try to find it?"

"I think I have to, don't I?" Shaw spoke in a hushed tone. "I mean, it's the only thing that's going to stop this from getting out of control. Already Silas is saying we have other things to worry about."

"The trolls." Rosalee leaned back in her seat. "Fucking trolls of all things."

"Oh, so you know already?" He nodded. "Oddest damn thing I ever heard. Something is really wrong in the world."

"Yeah, shortly after you met with Silas, Goldie came to find me. Silas summoned. He told me I get to put together my own team as if that's supposed to make it better." She scoffed. "Who the hell is going to want to tag along with me on that shit?"

"I thought you would be excited. This is a big deal and you get to head up the efforts to gather intel." Shaw glanced at Maze who was still working on his steak. Either he was really enjoying the bar food or he was working overtime trying to stay out of the conversation.

"Yeah, can't you see how I'm just full of energy and excitement over this?" Rosalee followed his eyes to the shadow walker and smirked.

"How do you contain yourself?" Shaw laughed.

"I'm going to go get a refill." Maze held up the empty glass despite the pitcher sitting on the table.

"Oh, shit, sorry we're being rude." Rosalee apologized. "I'm always talking off this guy's head whenever I get a chance to see him."

"No, you're catching up. Besides, it gave me time to stuff my face without worrying about holding a conversation." He winked and left the table.

"Does he know about the egg?" She asked after Maze left the table. She tapped the edge of the pitcher, still full of beer.

"I was about to tell him when you danced up to the table." Shaw nodded and she pulled a glass from thin air. "Where the hell did you have that? You know what, I don't want to know."

"Maybe you shouldn't tell him, at least not yet." She said as she filled her glass.

"What?" Shaw glanced over at Maze. "Why wouldn't I tell him?"

"It kinda paints the Peacekeepers in a bad light, you know."

"Like we need help with that." Shaw refilled his own mug.

"I'm just saying, be careful with what you share. Not everyone understands us."

"Maze isn't like that," he said. He knew what Rosalee was trying to do in her own indirect way. She was trying to protect him, keep him from getting hurt. "I can't explain it, but I know he doesn't judge people like that."

"He seems like a nice guy." She pointed to Maze, who was now chatting up Ral. "Won that old bird over already. And he doesn't feel as sketchy as other shadow walkers I've met."

"I admit I thought I would hate working with him. But Lee..." Shaw called her by the name he only used when he wanted to be vulnerable without judgement. It was a silent cue they agreed on with they were teenagers. "He had my back out there. Like I haven't had since—"

"I know." She poured another cup. "What are you going to do about him?"

"I wish I knew." Shaw thought about her question as the doors opened and Masto, the bear shifter and his diving team walked through the doors boasting about their catch. Moments later, music was playing and the rowdy crew already had a table overflowing with fresh beers.

"Shaw, I give you a lot of shit, I know. But I'm not doing that now. I see the way you look at him. I haven't seen that look in your eyes since Hank."

"Yeah well." He couldn't help but find Maze again. This time he was talking to Masto and once again it appeared he was making friends with one of the Keep's toughest residents.

"Well, what?" She asked. "It's mutual."

"What?" He turned back to her. "What's mutual?"

"Again, don't pretend like you don't know what I'm talking about here. Why else would he come all this way?" Rosalee stated the obvious and pushed the hair from her face.

"He says it's his fate to be a part of this." Shaw admitted. "I think he's nuts. If I had a choice, I wouldn't be tagging along to a potential fight with dragons."

"Fate, right? It might be his fate to be underneath you." She laughed.

"You are such a barbarian."

"Hey, you know I hang with the ogres. A girl is bound to pick up a few traits with them." She pulled her hair into a bun, anticipating Clifton, the shorter bear, planning to come bother her. Whenever the man saw her hair hanging free, it set something off within him. He wanted to touch it. The last time he tried, he nearly lost his hand.

"Not even ogres are that bad." Shaw shook his head and finished off the drink in his glass.

"Say what you want, but that man is here for more than slaying dragons."

Shaw looked over his shoulder at Maze, who now had another plate of food in his hand. He wondered where he got it and if he had to pay for it. "You think so, huh?"

"Yeah, I do." She stood. "Now, I'm going to get shit-faced because tomorrow I have to come up with a strategy to infiltrate the trolls and find out who their leader is."

"Have fun with that," Shaw said. "Don't drink too much. You

know how you get when you have a hangover."

"I'm a joy just as I always am!" She stuck her tongue out. "Don't miss me too much, big guy."

"What did I miss?" Maze returned to the table with a fresh pitcher and a plate with two new steaks as Rosalee danced away from them.

"Nothing, she is just getting her pre-trip buzz." He shook his head. "She's one of the best peacekeepers around, but she acts like a total fool most times."

"Maybe it makes the job easier to do." Maze offered. "I know that's how it was with Zanissa. Jokes got us through the muck, you know?"

"Yeah, maybe."

"So, you were going to tell me what the peacekeeper took?" Maze jumped right back into the conversation. "I figured you wanted to wait until we were alone to continue."

"Oh, yeah," Shaw thought about what Rosalee said, but went with his gut. If Maze was the sort to bow out of a trip because of the truth, he didn't want him on the trip at all.

"So, what was it?"

"An egg. Specifically, the queen's egg."

"Someone stole the Dragon Queen's egg?" Maze's jaw hung open. "Are you shitting me?"

"It's why we're so careful about who we let in now. Because some only wanted to use our access to the world to do unspeakable things. The decision of one asshole left all of Novia to burn."

"I take it you still believe this egg exists?" Maze started in on the next piece of steak.

"Yes, it's a valuable thing that hasn't turned up anywhere in the world. As long as it didn't break, which as you may know is extremely difficult to do, then we still have a chance to find it and return it to the queen." Shaw commented. They said the shell of a dragon egg to be more valuable than the child inside. It was durable and with magical properties that defied the laws of nature. An egg from the queen would have earned top dollar in the dark markets.

"You think giving her the egg back will fix everything?"

"I hope it will because right now, it's the only hope we have." Shaw finished his beer.

"I wonder how mad she is now. She's spent nearly a century in the ground." Maze speculated. "Then she wakes up, finds out she's lost all this time, and her egg is still lost."

"From the few seconds we saw her, I'd say she's pretty pissed off."

"Have you figured out what we're going to do next?"

"Yes, we're going to finish our food and drinks, then get some rest." Shaw looked down at his plate of cold food. "I don't know about you, but my brain is too tired to be planning how to hunt down a long-lost dragon egg right now."

"Fine by me. Besides, I made some new friends." Maze waved at the table of bears. "Might just want to go hang out with them a little more."

"Be careful of the little one, he gets handsy." Shaw said and a moment later heard Rosalee's fist crash into the bear's jaw. "One of these days he'll learn to keep his hands to himself."

THREE

When they made it back to Shaw's home, Maze was just as tipsy as Rosalee. The two ended up dancing together on in the middle of the bar and Masto, the bear, lifted Maze in the air as they cheered about whale steaks. Shaw half carried Maze back to his apartment and laughed as the shadow walker complained about the stairs, even though Shaw carried him on his back after the third flight.

Shaw only got Maze two steps inside the door before he was already stripping away the layers of clothes, now complaining about how hot he was.

"Why is it so warm in here?" Maze threw the shirt into Shaw's face. "I'm so tired."

"I would think so after all that singing and dancing." Shaw laughed as Maze flopped down on the couch. "You good to sleep here tonight?"

"This isn't the worst thing I've ever slept on." He fluffed up the pillow that sat on the couch.

"You can take the bed," Shaw offered. "I can sleep here."

"I'm fine here. I can take it." Maze flexed his arms. "Besides, you've been away from home the longest. Get your rest."

Shaw sat next to him. "I might have invested in something more comfortable if I knew I'd be having guests."

"This isn't exactly what I imagined life here to be like." Maze melted into the couch.

"What do you mean?" Shaw asked as he kicked off his boots. "Not cold enough for you?"

"No, that part is spot on, maybe even worse." Maze chuckled. "It's a lot more comfortable than I thought it would be."

"Is it?" Shaw yawned, the events of the day finally weighing on him. The bed in the other room was calling, and he was happy Maze hadn't taken him up on the offer of swapping places.

"Yes, and the bar. It was fun. Good food and decent music." He belched. "Never thought I'd be dancing with bears, you know?"

"Glad you enjoyed yourself." He smiled and watched Maze closely. He committed this moment to memory. The slight smile on his face, the way his eyelids hung low and his chest rose with each breath. There was so much more to Maze, and he wanted to know all he could. But he feared events wouldn't allow that. Shaw always gave Maze the option to leave. If he was honest with himself, he hoped he never would.

"You think they would let me come back to visit?" Maze words came slower with each passing minute.

"Okay, I know you didn't like it that much." Shaw raised a brow. "You're already planning your return?"

"Okay, maybe not but, we're... friends now, right?" Maze pointed out.

"Um, yeah, sure." Shaw fumbled.

"Don't over commit to the friendship." Maze laughed.

"Yes, we are friends." He nodded.

"Good. I don't know about you, but I like to keep up with my friends. Maybe even visit from time to time." Maze yawned. "Maybe in the warmer seasons, but yeah. I'd like to visit you again."

"We'll see how it goes. But this isn't really a place that welcomes visitors. Hell, we barely get news here. That isn't about some coming threat we need to take care of." Shaw said. "Most often we're leaving. The longest I've been home in the past few years is a week. And that might be a stretch."

"Well, with an angry Dragon Queen on the loose now, it might be a good time to switch things up a bit." Maze said. "Perfect time to have a friend to come and keep you grounded."

"I'll submit your suggestion to Silas for review." Shaw laughed.

"So, how does that work here? Silas is the boss and everyone reports to him?" He asked, and Shaw wondered how much of the conversation he could possibly retain.

"Unlike other places, the Keep works more like a democracy.

We voted for Silas for his position. We won't have another vote, however, unless someone steps up to take his place or he vacates it by choice or death."

"I take it no one is up for that position?" Maze asked. "Especially now with so much going on."

"No, and we believe in Silas. We trust his decisions."

"Too bad it's not like that in more places." Maze commented. "In Moon Hollow, we're just kinda stuck with the most powerful bloodline. Which is, of course, why Galari was so against Zanissa being with her vampire lover. That relationship would have destroyed the power of their bloodline."

"That is unfortunate." Shaw responded. "Love is hard to find. It shouldn't be a topic of regulation by anyone who isn't in the relationship."

"What's worse is that she made it sound like she just really wanted to protect her daughter, but we all knew the truth." Maze took a deep breath. "Zanissa felt like she was just a tool for her mother and I have to say that sometimes I wondered if she wasn't right."

"Do you ever plan to go back?" Shaw asked because it had been on his mind. The way Maze was so ready to continue with Shaw had more to it than a question of fate. Unlike Rosalee, Shaw didn't think that the connection had anything to do with a physical attraction to him.

"To Moon Hollow?" He asked.

"Yes," Shaw said. "Unless you have another home I don't know about."

"I hadn't thought about it." Maze turned those deep eyes on Shaw and he thought the man would start crying. "I mean, my mother is still there. I want to see her again."

"But you're not sure about returning home." Shaw spoke in a calm tone, hoping not to upset Maze.

"Look, the most important relationship in my life was Zanissa, and they took that away. I love my mother, but our relationship hasn't always been the greatest. I honestly worry that now that her debt is cleared, she is going to spiral out of control again."

"Maybe your being there will help keep her on the right path." Shaw suggested.

"Maybe, but I can't live my life trying to prevent her from destroying hers." Maze shook his head. "It's like punishing myself for her poor decisions. Trust me, I've taken enough hits already."

"That's actually a mature response to the situation."

"Well thank you, I do try to be mature." Maze looked at the window and smiled. "It's snowing. How is that it looks so peaceful? I know tomorrow will be worse because of it, but right now I couldn't imagine anything more beautiful."

"We should get some rest," Shaw stood and so did Maze, who was suddenly radiating nervous energy. "I'll get you something to sleep in and some bedding."

"Thanks, because I can already feel the chill setting in."

"The liquor wearing off. That's why most of us try not to get too drunk. If you get caught outside, it could mean freezing to death."

"Good to know." Maze dropped his head back on the couch. "For next time."

Shaw left him to retrieve the pajamas and covers for Maze. When he returned, he froze because Maze was standing in the living room, pulling his top off. The shadows of falling snowflakes moved across his skin and Shaw followed the path of those shadows with his eyes until he reached the top of the pants that sagged from Maze's hips.

"Um." He cleared his throat, averted his eyes, and held out the retrieved items. "Here you go."

"Thanks." Maze grabbed the stack from him.

"Let me know if you need anything else." Shaw looked at Maze's abs and chest. The man was in better shape than he thought for having such a slender frame. "I'm going to head to bed." He turned and walked away.

"Sleep tight." Maze called after him.

Usually, when Shaw laid down to rest, he fell right to sleep. It was something he bragged about. While others tossed and turned, struggling with their thoughts, he shut his brain off like a light switch. This night, with a shadow walker sleeping in the next room and the Dragon Queen out there organizing her people, he found it difficult to shut out the world and quiet his mind.

When he managed to sleep, he woke up with every sound. Worried that Maze would need him, he peeked out the door at him at least three times. And every time, his new friend was sound asleep.

It wasn't just the random noise that pulled him from sleep, either. It was also the recurring dreams of stolen dragon eggs and cities burning to the ground. Twice he woke up in a cold sweat and had to change his shirt before attempting to sleep again.

There was more that bothered Shaw. Everywhere he went, he heard the rumors, the whispers of changes to come to Novia. It spread across the world, reaching even the most untouched regions. The queen awakening felt like a trigger moment for everything they feared would happen. This was bigger than a mother upset over the loss of a child.

He hoped they could avoid it, that it would be like anything else. People would fear it, and in time forget all about it. That wasn't the case. Everything they saw, including the threat Silas saw in the trolls, made it clear that things were, in fact, about to change. Unfortunately, it didn't look like it was a change for the better.

His struggle continued for most of the night, but he did eventually find rest before the sun rose again. He wasn't one who typically slept in, but he planned for this day to be an exception. An explosion so big that it shook the walls ruined those plans.

Shaw jumped from his bed, fear that the dragon he'd just been dreaming of had somehow crossed over into reality. He paused, listening closely to make sure what he felt wasn't just a dream, and another explosion confirmed it was no dream. A series of screams followed the second explosion. The Last Keep was under attack.

Shaw ran from his room, jumping into his pants as he did, and came around the corner just in time to see Maze falling from the couch. He hit the floor, jumped up, and rubbed the side of his head that knocked against the nearby chair.

"What the hell was that?" Maze flickered as if jumping in and out of the shadow against the wall.

"I don't know." Shaw held his hands up. "You good?"

"Yeah, sorry, just startled me. Are we under attack? Are the dragons here?"

"I don't know, but I'm going to go find out." Shaw started gearing up for battle grabbing weapons from the closet by the door. "Stay here. If things get hairy, get the hell out of here."

"Shaw, I can help." Maze scrambled to dress.

"No, I mean it. If it gets bad, promise me you're going to shadow walk your ass out of here." Shaw repeated his concern. "This isn't your fight."

"Shaw," Maze started, but stopped speaking when the peacekeeper turned to look at him, eyes dark with concern.

"Maze, please." Shaw's heart pounded in his chest. He couldn't risk Maze getting hurt. He needed him to stay safe. "Don't make me beg you. Just take care of yourself. Please."

"Yeah, okay, I will." Maze backed down. "You do the same.

Don't go getting yourself killed out there."

Shaw hesitated for a moment, looking at the worry on Maze's face. He considered saying something more reassuring, but instead turned and left the room.

The attack was happening at the front gate. As he ran out of the building his apartment was in, he looked to the sky, expecting to find dragons flying overhead. But it was clear. If the attack didn't come from above, who was responsible for it?

"What's going on?" Shaw asked a man who ran by him.

"Trolls, fucking trolls!" The man shouted as he continued running.

"Fuck." Shaw muttered as he ran for the front gate. If they were being attacked, unprovoked, it meant they weren't prepared, and they needed support. He glanced up at the tower where Silas' home stood above the city. Where was their faithful leader in all of this?

Men ran to the front gates, all geared up with weapons, both modern and not. The Peacekeepers had guns and explosives, but they kept true to their roots. Every one of them still knew how to use a sword if times called for them.

Shaw preferred the old school method, get up close and personal, but of course he learned how to use the newer weapons as well. He made it to the wall and stepped inside the mechanical lift that took him to the top of the barrier platform.

When he reached the top, he ran to the edge where he got a

vantage point of the massive beings outside the walls. It wasn't many of them, enough to do damage but not enough to breakthrough. Their return fire had already cut the troll numbers down. Out of the three catapults aimed at their barrier wall, two were destroyed and trolls were already taking off running for cover. It wouldn't be long before they completely neutralized the threat.

"Get down there and get as many of those assholes as possible!" Silas ordered. As always, their leader was at the front line, defending their home. "I'll be damned if we're going to allow them a cheap shot and let the assholes get away without paying for this."

Moments later, peacekeepers on horses were in pursuit of the trolls who tried to get away. The last catapult fell and the members of The Last Keep cheered.

"You know what that was, right?" Shaw asked Silas while the others celebrated their victory.

"Yeah, they're feeling us out." Silas turned to him. "Which means they're going to attack soon."

"North wall is secure, this is the only attack point." Rosalee reported as she ran up to them. "This was a strategic move."

"You better move up your plans to head out." Silas ordered. "Get whatever team you need together and get out there. We need to make sure this doesn't happen again."

"Yeah, I'm on it." She huffed as she turned to leave, but stopped, then pointed at Shaw. "You might want to take care of the dragons. I mean odds are low that they would attack at the same time, but why chance it?"

"You're right. We will never survive simultaneous attacks." Shaw looked over the gate and watched as one troll was being dragged back to the Keep. They'd caught one, but the others were still headed back to their home with whatever intel they gathered. "We're leaving soon."

"You thinking of checking out the cave?" Silas asked.

"It's the logical first step. We've been there before, but maybe something changed." Shaw nodded. "Not sure what difference it will make."

"Maybe your shadow walker will see something you can't." Silas said and Shaw raised a brow.

"Hadn't thought of that. I guess that's always a possibility." He wanted to ask Silas more about his suggestion, but the leader was pulled away.

"Good luck." Rosalee told him before she too headed off to get her team together.

"Yeah, you too." Shaw nodded as he watched the cleanup happening on the ground below.

Shaw checked in with the men at the wall, making sure that everything was good before he headed back home. He had to make sure Maze knew they were safe. Stepping into the lift to return to the ground below, Silas joined him.

"Silas." He addressed him.

"Shaw, you good?" His leader looked out over their home as the lift engaged.

"Yes," Shaw confirmed. "Just a little shaken up. Not the best wake up call."

"Tell me about it. But hell, it's better than coffee, right?" Silas rubbed his hand over his bald head as they descended to the ground. "I can't believe this. It's been decades since anyone was bold enough to attack us here."

"At least this confirms what you were thinking. The trolls are angry with us." Shaw looked out the window at the body the men hauled in through the gates. "Any idea why they're so irritable?"

"I don't think it's the trolls. I think it's a bigger issue." Silas thought about what happened. "Listen, do you think you can handle this dragon thing on your own?"

"Why?" It wasn't typical for a Peacekeeper to go out on his own with an issue this big.

"We need as many people here as we can afford to have out. I'm calling back some of the scouts that are out now. You can always call in reinforcements when you need them."

"Yeah, that's good. Maze and I should be okay on our own for now. I'll keep you posted every step of the way. Let you know if I need backup." Shaw confirmed.

"Would be great if you didn't."

"What are the odds of that?" Shaw laughed, but if things went his way, he'd never have to call for help.

"You're right." Silas chuckled. "When do you plan to head out?"

"First light." The lift met the ground and Shaw opened the gate that kept them from falling out. "There are some things I need to get in order and I have to file my reports from the last trip."

"Good." Silas moved around. "Shaw?"

He stepped out of the lift. "Yes?"

"Be careful out there, I mean it. Things are changing fast. I need you to be safe." Silas stepped off the lift, and it moved back to the top of the wall. "Take every precaution and go with your gut. If shit gets iffy, get out."

"Will do."

"Good thing you got that shadow walker on your side."

"Why is that?" Shaw lifted the hood of this jacket over his locks.

"Well, if he is anything like his grandfather, he's powerful as hell." Silas looked to the sky as if seeing his friend's face. "That man saved me more times than I can count."

"So you had a close relationship with him?" Shaw asked. Silas made it seem as if he only vaguely knew the man, but clearly there was more to it.

"Yes, I did. Hell, if it weren't for him, Maryanna wouldn't have let me go on half the missions I went on." Silas laughed as he spoke of his late wife. "Keep that boy close to you."

"I'll do that." Shaw thought about how Maze had already saved him once before. He hoped like hell that this mission didn't call for more of that.

FOUR

"**M**aze, you still here?" Shaw asked as he stepped back into his home. The smell of food filled his nostrils. "Is that eggs I smell?"

"Hey, yeah. Things quieted down and I figured it was safe to stay." Maze held up a plate full of food. "You had bread and potatoes, but I asked your neighbor for a few eggs."

"I'll be sure to pay her back." Shaw looked at the plate and his stomach growled. The rush of adrenaline brought on by the explosions wore off and his sense of self-preservation returned.

"Such a sweet woman." Maze said as he placed two plates on the coffee table. Shaw didn't have a dining table and it wasn't often he ate at home. "So everything okay?"

"Yeah. I mean, not really." Shaw took his weapons off, putting them back in the closet. "But we've handled the immediate threat."

"Trolls, huh?" Maze asked. "Mrs. Leary told me that was what the commotion was. What did you guys do to piss them off? They're usually such gentle giants."

The trolls, while massive, the shortest being over nine feet tall, were exactly what Maze said, gentle giants. They lived in the far north in a community where they were one with nature. Anyone could visit as long as they meant no harm to the trolls. It was the opposite of any depiction Maze ever saw in the shows Zanissa's father brought back from Earth.

"That's what we're trying to figure out. Silas thinks someone else is behind it." Shaw sat down and started in on the plate. "This is good." He complimented Maze after his first bite.

"Someone is making the trolls attack you?"

"Yes, using them as weapons. As you know, trolls are powerful and hard to kill. They didn't use their magic to fight, though. They used weapons, which as far as we know, they wouldn't have access to."

"Interesting." Maze scratched his chin. "Looks like you've got a mastermind on your hand."

"Yeah, one who has it out for us, but we have no idea why. At least not yet. That's Rosalee's job to figure out."

"Sounds like a rather big problem to deal with." Maze worked on his own plate. "You think Rosalee can handle it?"

"Yes. She's one of the best we have." Shaw said confidently. "As much as I want to know what the hell is going on, this one is not our problem to think about, at least not right now. What we need to focus on is figuring out how to stop the dragons from joining the trolls in their attacks. The Keep will never survive something like that."

"What's your plan? Find the egg and get it back to the queen?"

"That's our best bet." Shaw confirmed. "Hope that we can find it and that returning it to her is enough for her to call off her men."

"Would it be enough for you?" The shadow walker asked. "If someone took your child from you, and on top of that stole a century of your life, is there such a thing as enough to make up for that?"

"I try not think about things in those terms." Shaw watched Maze. "I can't compare myself to these situations. We all have different motivators. Different reasons for why we do what we do. If I sit back trying to justify my actions like that, nothing will ever get done."

"Probably for the best, I think I'd still be ready to raise hell after being forced to sleep for a century and waking up to find that my child was still missing." Maze shoveled a spoonful of the potato hash in his mouth and spoke around the mouthful. "Any idea where we should start?"

"There is a cave at the base of Mt. Niccoli. We will have to get to the other side of the mountain to reach it."

"A cave?" Maze gawked. "As in a hole in the side of the mountain?"

"Yes. For a long time, we believed the egg might have been hidden there. We've checked it time and time again, never finding more than left over meals from bears."

"You want to go into a cave where you know bears have their meals to check for an egg that you already know isn't there?" Maze sat back from his plate. "This doesn't sound like a waste of time to you?"

"No. I don't think it's a waste of time. I think it's a good starting point. Maybe we'll see something there that they missed before. Maybe time has revealed something new." Shaw said. "Peacekeepers believed things are made known to us in their own time. Just because we were looking doesn't mean it was time for us to see."

"Ah, you're hoping it's time for you to see something new now?" Maze leaned forward, looking at Shaw closely.

"Yes, I am." Shaw sighed. "It's kind of the only hope we have right now. There are no other clues."

"Well, it looks like we're headed to the cave. Let's hope it's off season for the bears." Maze laughed. "When do we head out? I mean, not that I'm not loving my stay here."

"Ready to get out of the cold, huh?" Shaw chuckled.

"Yes!" Maze laughed. "I don't know how you do it here. Is it's like this all year round?"

"No, we get a few weeks in the late season that are seasonably warm."

"A few weeks?" Maze shook his head. "No, thank you."

"Well, you know, the mountainside can be a lot colder than

in the Keep. The wall actually radiates energy that warms up the inner city. At night, someone caught outside the walls may very well freeze to death."

"Let's not do that, huh?" Maze lifted a cup of water to his mouth. "I don't know how much more time I have in this world, but I don't want to leave it like that."

"I have no plans to do that." Shaw took a bite of his food and put a thumbs up in approval. "We'll leave out in the morning. I have a few things I need to take care of today. And apparently I need to replace some eggs for Mrs. Leary."

"I'm sure she will appreciate that." Maze dug back into the plate in front of him.

They finished eating and took turns in the shower before getting dressed to head out. Maze was thankful for the warmth of the water, but cursed the second he stepped out. While they had heat, Shaw explained that sometimes the system failed or relayed heat to areas that needed it more. With the attack on their barrier wall, the heat was being pushed to the areas where repairs were in progress.

Maze complained, but he understood. The layers of Shaw's clothing made up for the lack of warmth in the air.

As they moved through the streets of the Keep, Maze stuck close to Shaw. He was a quiet observer as he ran his errands, caught up with friends, and yes, purchased eggs to replace the ones borrowed from his neighbor. The older woman looked pleased just to know that Shaw was eating.

When they returned home, Maze meditated while Shaw worked on paperwork and plans for the next morning. There wasn't much the shadow walker could do to help. Later, he put some whale steaks in the oven and had cabbage boiling on the stove.

Mrs. Leary would be upset with him if he didn't make sure that Shaw ate well. At least that was the reasoning he gave for purchasing the meat at the market. Shaw didn't debate him on it. They needed a good meal before they left, and he wasn't interested in going back to the bar.

"You know, you really should try meditation. It's good for you." Maze said as he stretched his arms and legs. "With all the stress you're under now, it will help. Add some deep stretches and you'll lose that knot at the back of your neck."

"I meditate, or at least I used to." Shaw rubbed the back of his neck and frowned. How did Maze know it was there?

"Oh, when was this?" Maze asked as he squatted, stretching his lower back.

"Years ago. My partner, Hank. He was big on meditation and self-reflection." Shaw flipped over the page he was working on and continued writing his notes. "Something that's not the easiest to do when you're in my line of work."

"So you had a partner who you did missions with?" Maze asked, intrigued to learn more about Shaw.

"Um, yeah, something like that." Shaw hesitated to speak about the man who was no longer a part of his life.

"Oh, I'm sorry. I won't pry." Maze backed up from Shaw.

"You're not prying." Shaw looked him in the eye.

"Okay, good. So tell me more about this partner. Was he more than just a friend?"

"Yes." Shaw nodded. "He was."

"What happened to him?" Maze sat on the edge of the desk.

"He died." Shaw admitted.

"I'm so sorry." Maze put his hand over his mouth.

"It's okay. These things happen." He leaned back in his chair. "He got into a real awful fight with some vampires. They were suffering from sun sickness. He just stumbled onto them as they tried to hide from the sun. They saw him and they saw food. I beat myself up for a long time over his loss."

"Were you there?" Maze's voice was soft, hesitating as he asked more about Shaw's past.

"No, I wasn't there. That's the part I beat myself up over." Shaw looked out the window as he became lost in his own thoughts. "I was supposed to be. I took a different mission instead of sticking with him. Silas needed me for something else. Had I been there, he might still be here."

"I'm sorry for your loss, Shaw." Maze stood and put his hand on his shoulder. "Losing someone you love is never easy. I'm sure a lot of people have already told you this, but you can't blame yourself."

"Thanks." Shaw placed his hand on top of Maze's and looked up into his face. For a moment he couldn't think, but then he dropped his eyes, returning to the papers in front of him. "Well, our plan is done. I just have to file this with the registry and we'll be on our way."

"The registry?" Maze looked over his shoulder. "What's that?"

"It's like Silas' secretary. Documentation of missions is now a part of our standard protocol for all Peacekeepers. It's a precaution, so there is a record of every intended mission. I also have to file a report upon returning, which is what this second stack is for."

"That's a lot of work." Maze sucked his teeth. "Takes the fun out of the mission."

"They typically aren't all that fun, but it keeps us honest. Peacekeepers don't have the free rein we used to have."

"You miss it?"

"I might if I had been around during that time." Shaw laughed. "By the time I hit the field, this was the way things were done. Will you be okay here by yourself while I go file these?" Shaw asked.

"Yeah, absolutely. I'll just go hang out with Mrs. Leary again." Maze smiled. "You know, she really is a sweet old lady. Wouldn't expect someone as gentle as her to be a Peacekeeper. But then again, there's a lot about this place that is unexpected."

"You do that." Shaw stood from the table, gathered his forms and headed for the door but stopped and looked back at Maze. "Just don't borrow anything else."

On the third level of Silas' tower was the registry. Shaw entered the office as two butch men were walking out complaining about an unpleasant encounter with a bear shifter. Both were blaming the other for things going wrong.

He chuckled, remembering the days when he was stuck with a partner. Whenever something didn't go as planned, there was always the debate over who caused it. Whoever caused it had to file extra paperwork detailing what went wrong and how.

"Shaw," Birdie, a short redhead with large round glasses, greeted Shaw as he approached her desk. "It's always so nice to see you here."

Birdie had a deep voice with soft features and wore her hair in colorful braids that she styled in intricate ways. Her favorite, and the reason she got her nickname, was a bird's nest. Today, however, she had it styled like a waterfall in various shades of blue.

"Thanks, Birdie." Shaw smiled. "It's good to see you, too."

"How was your trip?" She said, around the toothpick in her mouth. "Good things found?"

"I wish I could say that. Actually, I'll be headed out again tomorrow." Shaw held up the two individual packets for her to file.

"Oh, so you're bringing me double the work." She pressed her hand to her large chest and pouted. "I thought you loved me, Shaw."

"I do. I swear it." He pulled a small baggie of cinnamon candies from his pocket. It was her favorite, and he always picked her up some when he went to the market.

"Oh, you do love me. Well, since you brought me such goodies, I'll forgive you for all these nasty forms I have to file."

"Thank you. You're so sweet."

"Kissing up again, I see." Rosalee spoke from behind him.

"Hey, I'm just making sure our Birdie is well taken care of." Shaw winked at the woman behind the desk and she blushed.

"Sure, filling her with cinnamon treats."

"Hey Rosalee." Birdie waved.

"Hey, sweets." Rosalee waved and pulled her own bag of treats out of her pocket.

"And you talk about me." Shaw pointed to the bag. "Hypocrite."

"Hey, like you said, we have to take care of our Birdie." Rosalee handed Birdie her departing forms, then turned back to him. "You tell him about the egg?"

"Wow, straight to digging for dirt. Not even a formal hello." He shook his head and leaned against the desk. "If you must know, yes, I told him."

"And?" She leaned against the desk where Birdie sat, peering over her glasses, clearly interested in the tea that Rosalee spilled all over her desk.

"And what?" Shaw winked at Birdie, who then pretended to be engrossed in her work.

"How did he take it? Is he still here or did he freak out and run back to Moon Hollow?"

"He's still here, and no, he didn't freak out." He paused, thinking about the man in question. "I told you, he's not that type of person."

"Well, color me surprised." Rosalee grabbed him by the shoulder, pulling him in close to whisper in his ear. "Don't let this one get away."

"You're ahead of yourself, Rosalee." He pushed her away and bumped his shoulder against hers. "Good luck on your trip."

"Same to you. Makes sure you two keep warm on that mountainside. You know it's best to share body warmth." She poked him in the side as she danced out the door. "I'm going for drinks. Who wants to buy me a drink?" She called out into the hall full of peacekeepers.

"That woman is amazing." Birdie commented, and when Shaw looked at her, she coughed. "But she doesn't even compare to you, of course."

"You'll tell me anything for more candies." Shaw tapped the table with his hand. "Take care, I'll see you next time."

"One set of forms please." Birdie called after him as he headed out of the office.

FIVE

Shaw had a better night's sleep than before. It could have been because of the good meal he ate. Or the stretching that Maze insisted he did before going to bed. Either way, he slept comfortably and woke up well-rested and ready to hit the road before the sun came up.

"I know you said first light, but this is a little intense." Maze looked out the window. The light of the sun just barely peeked over the horizon.

"I figured it would be faster for us to shadow walk most of the way. This way it gives you ample to work with. And we avoid any hungry predators that live on the mountainside." Shaw pointed to the range in the distance.

"Smart." Maze yawned. "Still, very early."

Again Maze showered, cursing the temperature when he stepped out into the chilly air. Shaw handed him new clothes to wear and packed their bags with rations for the road. It would be at least two days before they had access to fresh food. The mountain offered little to be eaten that didn't need to be slaughtered first.

Shaw had Maze wait until they were outside of the Keep's border wall before they stepped into the shadows. He wanted to keep the trust of the other peacekeepers. And when they stepped into the darkness, it was even colder than the already frigid temps. Maze pulled Shaw through the shadows faster than he ever had. Luckily, Shaw was already comfortable following Maze in the dark space.

"Dammit." Maze shook his legs and arms as they stepped into the light from the shadows. "Why is it so damn cold here?"

"You want to rethink that whole visitation idea?" Shaw laughed at his display. It was definitely cold, but the peacekeeper was used to the temperatures.

"Yeah, I might," Maze said. "Or come up with some magical way to wrap an invisible blanket of heat around me."

"That's right, shadow walkers don't have the same powers as the other witches, right?"

"Right. We have limited use of magic. Nothing nearly as powerful as what Zanissa would be able to do." Maze rubbed his hands over his arms.

"You think you'll ever see her again?" Shaw asked. The way Maze talked about his best friend, he didn't think she was dead, but wherever she was, he couldn't get to her.

"No. Not after what her mother did. Where she is, it's even colder than it is here." His expression turned somber and Shaw kicked himself for asking the question.

"Sorry to hear that." Shaw turned and scanned the side of the mountain, pointing ahead of them. "There is the cave up ahead. I'll go in first to make sure there isn't anything living inside currently."

"I appreciate your sacrifice!" Maze called out to him, who already started walking to the cave. "Hopefully there are no bears."

"Hey, I have to keep you safe. You're my ride." He waved his hand above his head, not looking back.

"Your ride, huh? I'll give you a ride alright." Maze retorted, then froze awkwardly.

Shaw looked back at him with a raised brow, but Maze looked away. Shaw considered saying something, but thought better of it and instead continued his escape of the awkward moment.

He entered the cave carefully, checking for bears or any other animal that might want to kill them. He hadn't told Maze, but bears weren't the worst thing that had to worry about. Mt. Niccoli had recently become home to a family of Laugeros. An animal closely related to the lions of earth but twice the size and with paralyzing venom. The animal was typically found in the far north, but had recently migrated. The freezing temperatures were great for their thick furs.

"It's clear," he came out and told Maze, waving him to come into the cave, but he wasn't there. "Maze?"

"Good." Maze said from behind him, stepping out of the shadows.

Shaw jumped, then turned to him, dagger drawn. "Dammit, Maze. Don't do that."

"Sorry." Maze looked at the knife still pointed at his neck. "You going to cut me with that?"

"Not this time." Shaw lowered the knife. "But I wouldn't recommend doing that again."

Maze bowed to the peacekeeper. "I appreciate your restraint."

"I'm feeling generous." He put his dagger away. "We need to look around, see what we can find."

"And the egg is supposed to be hidden somewhere in here?" Maze started scanning the space. There wasn't much to see at first, but the deeper he went, he saw three tunnels branching off at the back of the cave. "Um, you're sure there's nothing down here?"

"Yes, those tunnels all end within thirty feet." Shaw reassured him. "There's nothing to be worried about. And yes, we thought we would find the egg down here, but never did. I'm not even sure how the rumor started that the damn thing was here, but it's all we have to go on."

"So, we need to look deeper." Maze touched the wall of the cave and inhaled deeply.

"Meaning?" Shaw asked, walking closely behind Maze.

"Maybe we're not supposed to be looking for an egg. Maybe it's a clue to where to find the egg."

"We thought about that too, but still we found nothing." Shaw shook his head. "There isn't much to this place. One room with three tunnels that lead to nothing."

"You mind if we walk the tunnels?" Maze turned to Shaw.

"You want to walk each one?"

"You have somewhere else to be?" Maze asked.

192

"No, I guess I don't." Shaw held his hand out, ushering Maze down the first tunnel. "After you."

Maze headed down the first tunnel on the right. He took careful steps as the further they went into the tunnel, the less light there was.

"I have a light," Shaw offered.

"No, something tells me that whatever is in here is something that can't be seen in the light. Besides, I'm more comfortable with the dark."

"Whatever you say." Shaw stayed as close to Maze as possible, just in case.

They made it to the back of the tunnel but found nothing new. Just like Shaw said, there wasn't much to the place except a pile of bones that Maze almost tripped over on his way out.

"I thought you were more comfortable in the dark," Shaw said after saving Maze from face planting.

"Hey, being more comfortable doesn't mean I can't still be a little clumsy from time to time." Maze straightened himself. "With you by my side, I'm safe from even my own stumbles."

"On to the second tunnel."

"Yes, we must keep on task." He saluted Shaw and headed for the middle tunnel.

In the second tunnel, they found the same thing. A long narrow space with nothing more than a few leftover carcasses from whatever was the animal that made it their home last. They examined the space carefully, making sure to not look over anything. But again, they found nothing of value.

"Third times the charm?" Maze frowned as he exited the second tunnel, this time without tripping over himself.

"Let's hope so." Shaw chewed his lip and looked back at the opening to the cave. Just because nothing was there when they got there doesn't mean they didn't have to worry about something showing up while they were there.

They reached the back of the last tunnel, once again coming up with nothing. Just as Maze turned to leave he paused.

"Wait, I feel something." He grabbed Shaw's shoulder, and they froze.

"What is it?" Shaw tried to look around, but he was as good as blind in the back of the space.

"There is something in the darkness, a low hum of electricity." He turned back, looking deeper as he tried to figure out what it was.

"Is everything okay?" Shaw asked. He could feel Maze's energy shift.

"I need to go into the shadows." Maze answered him. "I think there is something in there."

"What? Are you sure?"

"Yes, I don't know what it is but I feel something, kinda like a low buzzing." Maze sucked his teeth. "Whatever it is, I won't figure it out while standing out here."

"Do you want me to come with you?" Shaw offered.

"No, I want you to stay out here and make sure that no bears come back to eat me on my way out." Maze joked.

"Gotcha." Shaw said. "Just be careful."

~~*~~

Maze stepped into the shadows and at first, he saw nothing, but he could still feel that low hum of electricity. As he crept through the darkness, he realized it wasn't electricity he felt. It was something else, something familiar–a signature.

When he was a young boy, his grandfather always talked about how he signed his shadows. Some shadow walkers made this a thing years before Maze was born. It was like leaving behind a calling card. A message to any other shadow walkers that walked the path after you. They used it to tell stories of their travels and warn other people if it was a dangerous path to be on.

Being a shadow walker wasn't a guarantee. You had to be born into a family of shadow walkers, and even then it was a wait and see moment. Only men were true shadow walkers, though there were some women, like Tenia, one of the guardians of Moon Hollow, who found a way to use her magic to walk in great distances through darkness. But there was a difference between manipulating the space around you and actually becoming one with the shadows.

Most men came into their abilities when they reached puberty, but Maze was different. He started shadow walking at age six. He could still remember his mother's screams as he stepped out of the shadows in the kitchen as she was cooking dinner. She spilled soup all over the floor and it took her an hour to clean up the mess.

Shortly after he developed his ability, his grandfather taught him about shadow signatures. He said he wanted him to know how it felt to be familiar with the touch, the sound, even the taste of it. Yes, a shadow walker's signature could alter the taste of the air.

What Maze felt in the shadow, humming against his flesh in the moment, was the remnants of his grandfather's signature. The closer he got to it, he could no longer deny it. The closer he got to the source, the louder the noise and the more intense the feeling was that raced across his skin. It was just like he remembered it. Hairs standing on his arms, he kept going.

Every shadow had an end. Where there was a fold in space that a shadow walker used to cross into new areas. At the very back of this shadow, just before the fold, was something hidden where only he could see. A small envelope wrapped in silver wire. It was the only element that could be seen inside the shadows.

Maze looked at the envelope as he considered if it was smart to pick it up. He didn't think it was a trap. If it were, his grandfather wouldn't have hidden it in the shadows. Of course, no other peacekeeper had ever found it. They needed a shadow walker to get it, and it wasn't often that the two made alliances. But from the discovery of the envelope, he knew it wasn't the first time.

That envelope with that signature meant at some point in time his grandfather walked into that cave. It was a strategic move, putting a clue to a horrible puzzle in one place most could never look.

Already he had so many questions, like why his grandfather chose that cave. Who was he working with? And was this the reason he made sure Maze could recognize his signature? When he was older, he asked his mother about the signature and she knew told him she didn't know what he was talking about. Yeah, she knew about shadow signatures, but his grandfather didn't say much to her about it. Maybe he didn't trust her to know more.

He realized the shadows would provide no answers to his question and picked up the envelope. Once it was in his hands, he had the feeling of familiarity again. It told him he was on the right path. Yes, there was more to his grandfather than he knew, but somehow the old man knew he would be in that tunnel with a Peacekeeper.

He turned to leave the shadows, but then his mind flooded with a new line of concerns. Maybe his grandfather left the envelope where no one could find it for a reason. Maybe it was best that it remained hidden. This hadn't been the first secret his grandfather entrusted to him.

But then again, if he didn't want it to be found, he could have just destroyed it. Either way, Maze knew there was no way that he could leave it there with all of Novia at risk. And above everything else, he trusted Shaw. He couldn't explain it, but he trusted that man with his life, even though he'd only known him for a short time.

With the envelope tucked safely in his pocket, Maze stepped out of the shadows.

~~*~~

"Thank god," Shaw said as he felt Maze's energy return from the shadows. "Are you okay?"

"Yes, I'm okay, sorry it took so long." He apologized. "Had to go a little further than I thought I would."

"Don't worry about it. Did you find anything?" Shaw was nervous. He couldn't see Maze, but he knew something about the man was different. How could he have changed in such a short time?

"Yes, you can turn the light on now." Maze spoke.

197

Shaw pulled the small orb from his pocket and activated the light by tapping it with the tip of his finger. It gave just enough light so they could see each other.

"What do you find?" Shaw asked.

"This." Maze pulled the envelope from his pocket and showed it to him.

"An envelope? Someone hid an envelope in the shadows?"

"Yes, and I think this is what you've been looking for all these years. Only whoever put it here wanted to make sure the right person found it. There was no way any of you would have found it without a shadow walker who knew the signature."

"Maze, what is it?" Shaw could tell he was holding something back by the way he chewed on his bottom lip. "Was there something else in there? Did you get hurt?"

"No, I didn't get hurt, but there is something else I think I need to tell you." Maze hesitated. Something in his eyes told Shaw that he was afraid. But why would he ever be afraid of him?

"Whatever it is, tell me. You can trust me." Shaw grabbed his hand to comfort him. There was something Maze was struggling with.

"Shadow walkers can leave a signature in the shadows. It's not something widely practice as most people in the shadows are in there because they don't want to be found. But they can do it. The signature in that shadow, I felt it because I know it. I've known it for most of my life." Maze admitted.

"You do?" Shaw looked over Maze's shoulder to the shadows. "Who does it belong to?"

"It's my grandfather's signature." He almost choked on the words.

"Are you sure?" Shaw looked at the envelope again and then back to Maze.

"Yes, I'm sure. There aren't that many true shadow walkers anymore. You know we're a dying breed. When I started shadow walking, before I could even read, my grandfather taught me his signature. He would leave it in random places and inside the shadows, wrapped in silver wire, would be a treat or a gift for me." He held up the envelope, wrapped in that same silver wire.

"I know his signature better than I know my own, Shaw. My grandfather was here. He was in this cave almost a century ago with a Peacekeeper. Or maybe he came alone. Maybe he acted on his own, but I think he hid it here so that I could find it. That just leaves only one question. How could he have possibly known I would be here?"

"Maze, calm down." Shaw looked him in the eyes. "You said that someone gave you a message about how you were meant to be on this journey, right?"

"Yes." Maze took a deep breath. "She said my journey was one that would impact the world."

"Could it be possible that the same person who gave you that message also spoke to your grandfather? Or maybe it was a different person, but the message was the same." Shaw rationalized. "He had a fate, a destined journey, just like you did. Maybe hiding that envelope here for you was a part of his fate."

"Do you think…" Maze paused as if not sure he would continue.

"Do I think, what?" Shaw touched his shoulder. "What is it, Maze?"

"Do you think my grandfather could have had something to do with this? Is it possible that he actually helped steal the egg? I mean, I really don't want to believe that he could be responsible for something like that, but how else can I explain this? How else would he have known about this?"

"Those are questions we won't figure out here. And it's not good to speculate on things like that. Trust me, it will send you spiraling out. I've been there."

"You're right. I know you are." Maze looked at the envelope in his hand. "What's next? Do we open it?"

A noise in the cave caught Shaw's attention. He lifted his hand, warning Maze not to speak. Low growls bounced around the tunnel as the massive beast appeared at the end of the tunnel. The light from the orb revealing to him two meals ripe for the picking. The large teeth of the laugeros.

"Time to leave?" Maze asked.

"Yes, definitely."

Maze placed his hand on Shaw's shoulder and together they carefully stepped out of the tunnel and into the shadows.

SIX

Out of the shadows and in a safe location far away from the cave with the hungry predator, Maze and Shaw sat together beneath two trees. He'd walked them through the shadows out of the frigid temperatures and into the warmth of Lesera, a forest filled with rose-colored trees.

"Finally, my toes can thaw out." Maze looked up at the sun above them.

"Yeah, I'm accustomed to the cold, but even I can appreciate the warmth of the sun." Shaw dropped the bag on the ground before he turned to find Maze staring at the envelope. "Are you going to open it?"

Maze looked down at the envelope in his hands. He flipped it over a few times, examining it. "I know I should, but there's something about this envelope that is making me hesitate."

"Understandable, but..." Shaw recognized the frown on Maze's face. "What's wrong?"

"Nothing, it's just..." He held the envelope up for Shaw to see. "The envelope was blank before. Plain, white, and wrapped in

201

silver, right?"

"Yes, it was." Shaw looked at the envelope, no longer plain but with a symbol on the front. "Light-activated ink. We use it a lot."

"So we have a special peacekeeper light-activated ink used to write on this envelope in my grandfather's hand." Maze tapped the front of the envelope where a small symbol appeared. A triangle with a line down the middle was the symbol of the shadow walkers.

"I know it's the shadow walker symbol, but how do you know your grandfather wrote it?"

"Because of the way it's written." Maze scrutinized the writing. "If there was any doubt about my grandfather's involvement, this eliminates it. He drew it just like this. Usually, it's just a straight line, but if you look at the bottom of the line, there's a small arrowhead. It was another way that my grandfather made himself stand out. And another thing that he made sure I knew about him."

"I think that proves that they meant for you to find this." Shaw nodded. "I know it's a hard thing to accept, but I don't think there is any more room for denial."

"Yeah, and there's something else." Maze bit his bottom lip.

"Tell me, what is it?"

"The last time I saw the symbol, it was on another envelope, just like this one. The letter inside led me to another hidden discovery. I haven't even opened the damn thing and I already know there is a connection between the two."

"The only way we're going to figure that out is if you open it." Shaw couldn't help himself. He was eager to find out the message inside the envelope. His people had waited so long to get even close to the truth about what happened. There it was, in Maze's hands, and the man couldn't bring himself to open it. "I know that you're struggling with this, but time is not on our side. Whatever is inside of the envelope, we need to know what it is. We need to make sure that we're on top of this."

"You're right." Still, Maze just stared at the envelope.

"Do you want me to open it?" Shaw offered.

"No. No, I can do it." Maze waved his empty hand, rejecting his offer. "I should do it. Like you said, he clearly meant for me to be the one to find it. I have to be brave enough to at least open it."

He took a deep breath, then removed the silver string wrapped around the envelope. He slipped his finger under the flap of the envelope and quickly opened it. Inside was a piece of paper. He unfolded it, and as the sunlight touched the page, it revealed a message written in the same ink as the envelope.

Maze gasped as he saw his name appear first on the page.

Mazeviun,

It's only been a few weeks since you took your first step into the shadows. Just as the witch predicted. And if she was right about that, she was right about this. It is your duty to protect what was stolen, just as it was mine. Only I can no longer fulfill my duties. Old age and too many shadow walks have made me tired.

You are in the right place, but I cannot be sure that you will be the one to find this letter. That is why I left you the other clues. If you followed them, then you already have what you need. If you didn't, well, you better high tail it because time is running out. The egg still exists. It's somewhere safe, but you, with the help of your friends, need to find it and keep it safe until she is ready for it.

Love you, kiddo, and as always,

Walk safely into the shadows.

-Pops

"So he didn't steal the egg, he was protecting it."

"That's good." Shaw smiled.

"I know it's crazy, but it means something to me to know that I'm not related to the type of person who would do something like that." Maze shook his head. "Trust me, I have enough family karma to deal with."

"It's not crazy at all." Shaw placed his hand on Maze's knee. "Our legacies mean something, just as much as our origins. It seems like you were really close to your grandfather."

"I was. Childhood wasn't the best for me. Now and then, he would step out of the shadows and for a moment, things would be better." Maze's eyes watered. "I used to stare into corners hoping I would see him appear."

"I'm sorry you had a rough childhood. I can relate to that."

"Being raised by Peacekeepers wasn't a thrill ride?" Maze looked at Shaw and his heart broke for the man.

"No, not at all." Shaw sighed. "It was hard, full of endless training, physical and emotional trauma, and sleepless nights wondering why I didn't have parents."

"What do you mean you didn't have parents?" Maze tucked the letter back into the envelope and slipped it into his pocket. "What happened to them?"

"Peacekeepers who are born in the Keep, are raised in the Saget. It's like a boarding school. They place the kids there six weeks after birth. We never know who our parents are." Shaw thought back to his own childhood and how many times he tried to pick his parents out in the crowd. "Doesn't stop you from trying to figure it out though. I had a lot of imaginary parental bonds that shattered in my face."

"That sounds horrible. I guess there are negatives on both sides of it." Maze said. "Some of us long for our parents, while others wish they could escape them."

"Yes, there are." Shaw paused to breathe. This wasn't the conversation he wanted to have. "Okay, we need to get back to trying to figure this out. We still don't know what happened."

"Yeah, you're right." Maze blinked, forcing his own tears to subside.

"Did you ever do what the letter asked you to?" Shaw asked. "Did you follow the clues?"

"Yes, I did." Maze nodded.

"What did you find?" Shaw was relieved. It meant they wouldn't lose time backtracking.

"A series of envelopes like this one that led me to the Maistrier where I spoke to Riza." Maze reported. "It took a lot to get there, but I did it."

"Really? Few people have been there." Shaw looked impressed. "Most give up before they even get close."

"Yeah, that place is a total mind fuck. Not sure how he lives there without going crazy."

"Maybe he is crazy, and we just don't know it." Shaw pointed out. "Last time I was there, he kept rambling about bird feeder designs."

"Okay, that's interesting."

"It really isn't." Shaw laughed. "So, you got whatever was stored in the Maistrier?"

"I did. And I didn't know what it was. All I knew was that I was supposed to keep it safe. Riza said it couldn't stay there, in a secured underground layer. That its place was with me."

"Was it another envelope?"

"No, a box. Same symbol on the front."

"What's inside the box?"

"That I don't know. I could never get it to open, not that I tried all that hard to figure it out. I guess it would be helpful if I had, but I was just nervous about what I might find inside. Nothing good ever came out of a box that had that much power keeping it closed. I definitely didn't think I would find anything related to a stolen dragon egg."

"You're still doubting your grandfather's motives, aren't you?" Shaw watched the shadow walker closely.

"Yes, I hate to admit it, but I am. This says I'm supposed to protect this thing, but how did he get involved?"

"Maze, we don't know what happened. And I know that this is upsetting, but just keep in mind that your grandfather was a great guy. Until this point, you've had no reason to doubt him. Don't change that based on some inconclusive evidence. For all, we know your grandfather is the reason that egg didn't hit the black market or fall into the hands of some evil warlock. Hopefully, wherever it is, it is still safe and we can get it back. Because if we don't..."

"Yeah, I know if we don't all of Novia will burn." He said with a heavy sigh.

"Are you going to be okay?" Shaw placed his hand on Maze's shoulder.

"I think so. I mean, it sucks, but what else can I do?"

"We're going to get the box and figure out how to open it and we're going to keep moving until we can't anymore. That's all we can do at this point: keep fighting, keep pushing, and hoping for the best." Shaw waited for Maze to look at him. "There's a different now, you know that, right? I'm here for you. As you said, we're friends now. I'm going to help you through this, because that's what friends are for."

"Yeah, you're right." Maze placed his hand over Shaw's. "I don't think I could face this alone. I'm glad you're here."

"I'm here as long as you want me to be." Shaw smiled and his heart warmed again when Maze returned the expression. "So, where is the box? Hopefully, we can open it."

"I don't know if you're gonna like my answer to that question." Maze chuckled.

"Why is that?" He asked, worried about the answer.

"It's in Moon Hollow," Maze started. "Let me preface this by saying I didn't understand how important this thing was."

"Meaning?" Shaw waited for him to provide more clarity as to where the box was.

"Meaning it may not exactly be in the safest location either." Maze rubbed his hand over his face. "I mean, considering all that my grandfather went through, I should have found a better place for it, but I just went with what felt safest at the time."

"Oh no." Shaw feared the worst, hoping it wasn't sitting out on a mantel somewhere.

"It's–"

Shaw held up his hand. "No, don't say it out loud. Call me

208

paranoid, but I'd rather you just take me there."

"You think someone is lurking in the woods trying to eavesdrop on our conversation?"

"I think I've been around long enough to know that you can never tell what's gonna happen. People have spies everywhere and if you don't need to say something aloud, don't."

"You're the expert here." Maze agreed. "Can we eat something before we go? I'm starving."

"Yes, of course." Shaw pulled the bag from his back and unpacked the food for them to eat.

They sat, sharing stories about their lives as they ate the rations Shaw provided. When they were done, they packed up, being careful not to leave a mess behind. There were creatures in the Lesera, that were so bonded to the forest that they would kill anyone who dared to disrespect it. Dark beings that rose from the ground and pulled anyone who harmed their home to a suffocating death.

Once cleaned up, Maze lead them into the shadows, and off to Moon Hollow.

SEVEN

Maze avoided the gates and used the shadows to carry them straight to his home. It was better to avoid any potential contact with Tenia and her guards. They still weren't sure what they were up against, and both agreed that having to explain a clue about a dragon egg that most people hadn't known about wasn't something either of them wanted to deal with.

"This is your house?" Shaw whispered, afraid someone would hear him.

"Yes, it is." Maze nodded. "Home sweet home."

They stood outside of the house under the cover of the coming night. Light shone in the cottage window. Someone was home.

"Are we going to go in?" Shaw asked. "Do you want me to stay outside?"

"Yes, I mean, I don't know why I'm nervous about." Maze shook his head. "We're just here to grab the box and go."

"You afraid of me meeting your mother? I can always sneak in the back."

"That won't be necessary." Maze laughed nervously. "This would be the first time I've ever brought anyone home with me, though. I mean, not that this is like taking a boyfriend home to meet Mom. It's just the only reason my mom knew Zanissa was because of her status in Moon Hollow. I was always too afraid for people to know her."

"And embarrassed?" Shaw recognized that look on Maze's face. It was the same one he wore when anyone confronted him with topics he'd rather not discuss.

"Yes, that too. I was the son of the crazy drunk with mountains of debt that would leave our family in ruins. It was hard enough just living life without being seen with her. As I got older and she cleaned her act up. I hated myself for feeling that way, but it's still there. Every day, I fear she will slip up and once again become the woman who made my childhood a living hell."

"Is there any way we can get inside and not have her know?" Shaw asked as he checked out the brick building. It looked solid, no way to get in or out without being seen.

"No, my mom can't shadow walk, but she could always feel it when I did it in the house. She probably knows I'm out here now." Maze shrugged. "If she does, she won't wait much longer before she comes out here."

"So no sense waiting out here then." Shaw walked up to the door, knocking before Maze could stop him.

"Wait," Maze said too late.

"Now we wait," Shaw said.

They stood there for a few minutes, but here was no answer.

"Should I knock again?"

"No, if she were here, she would have answered." Maze relaxed. "Which means we can get in and out of here without worrying about you being accosted by my mother."

"Maybe next time."

Maze lifted his finger, touching it to the lock on the door. Witches used spells to secure their home. This one recognized Maze and gave him access to the home. He pushed the door open, then froze in a panic. As the door moved, it revealed the inside of the house was completely wrecked. The furniture had been overturned and there were things, artifacts of his childhood, tossed all over the floors.

"Let me go in first." Shaw said and headed in the house ahead of Maze, who was still frozen in shock. He did a quick inspection of the house, finding no one else inside, then returned to Maze. "There's no one here, but whoever came here was looking for something."

"Do you think they knew about the box?" Maze looked from the mess on the floor.

"I doubt it. We only found out about it a little while ago." Shaw reasoned. "If anyone knew about it, they would have come a long time ago."

Maze walked into the house. "My mom."

"She's not here." Shaw held up his hand. "The place is empty."

"What the hell happened here?" Maze tiptoed around the mess. "Who could have done this? Why would they do this?"

A knock pulled both their attention to the front door where a chubby man stood peaking inside the house. Maze quickly walked over to the guest.

"Maze, I wasn't sure if I would see either of you here again." The older man glanced at Shaw then back to Maze.

"Hastings." Maze greeted him. "Do you know what happened here?"

"Oh, no one told you?" The older man shook his head. "Your mother, she fell off the wagon and onto a downward spiral like I haven't seen before. She ran up a debt again, this time it was with the wrong person."

"Not the Licone?" Maze asked.

"No, I don't think they would have ever given her anything else." Hasting scratched his chin through the thick gray beard. "Never seen these people before. New crew and they looked strange. They came, took everything they could, and left. I would have come over to help, but your mom wasn't here when it happened. Not sure where she is, but I assume it's far from here."

"Thanks, Hastings." He shook the man's hand.

"I'm sorry, Maze. We were all hoping this time she would stay good."

214

"Yeah, me too." Hastings left and Maze closed the door.

"I'm sorry." Shaw said. "The Licone are tough. I didn't realize your mother had that kind of debt."

"It's fine. Right now, we need to make sure that they didn't get that box." Maze turned and headed for his room.

They also trashed his room, all of his stuff was over the floor. He dropped to the floor, looking under the bed, and reached into the darkness. A moment later, he turned to Shaw and smiled.

"I don't think they got it. Help me move the bed?"

Shaw helped Maze move the bed from the wall. He knocked on the wall near the baseboard and it popped open. He reached into the wall and pulled out a black satchel.

"It's in there?"

"Along with everything else I value. I could never trust my mother not to sell off all my stuff to support her habit. There were days when I would come home to most of my clothes missing. I thought of using the shadows, but like I said, she could feel it. And she knew people who could and would enter the shadows to steal from me."

Maze opened the bag, pulling out the box with the symbol of the shadow walkers on it.

"This is it." He handed it to Shaw.

"Now we just need to figure out how to open it." Shaw

examined the box.

"Yes, but not here. I don't doubt that whoever did this is still watching the place." Maze took the box back and stuffed it in the bag. He also grabbed a few other items and some clothing to change into. "We need to get out of here."

"Through the shadows?" Shaw watched Maze and tried to remain calm because he could tell Maze was on the edge.

"Yes." Maze nodded and reached for Shaw, but he pulled back.

"Wait."

"What am I waiting for?" Maze asked, confused.

"Are you sure you want to go now? If you want to stay, and help your mom–"

"No, I can't. I need to do this." Maze struggled with the decision. "Besides, I did all I could for her. I agreed to go with you so I could help her. How long has it been? A couple weeks since I left, and she's already racked up so much debt that she's on the run and our home has been destroyed. There is nothing I can do for her now. This is what's important. Figuring out how to open this box so we can find that damn egg."

He stood, tucked the satchel into the bag he already carried, and held his hand out to Shaw.

"Alright, let's go." Shaw nodded, took his hand, and a moment later, the two stepped into the shadows to leave.

When they exited the shadows, they were on the outside of the wall that stood around Moon Hollow.

"I can't believe–" Maze started, but Shaw held his hand up stopping his rant prematurely.

"Someone's here." Shaw warned.

"Are you sure?"

"Yeah, I'm sure." Shaw pointed in the distance where a Cisk riding an aerohorse appeared.

"You think they're here just to say hello?" Maze asked, but they both knew the answer to that question.

"Well, I don't have any personal relationships with Cisks, what do you think?" Shaw glanced over his shoulder at Maze.

"I think we better be careful here." Maze tightened the bag on his shoulder.

"Peacekeeper?" The Cisk addressed them.

"Can I help you?" Shaw looked up at the Cisk who still sat on his horse.

"Yes, I believe you have received something we need." The Cisk spoke from beneath the helmet. "Hand it over and we'll be on our way."

"You're going to have to give me a little more information here." Shaw played dumber. "What exactly is it that you think I have?"

"No one knows, but what we do know is that it's in that bag." They pointed to the bag Maze carried. "We're going to need that."

"Like hell you are." Maze refused him.

"What you have is powerful, more powerful than you can handle. Hand it over and we'll make sure it's taken care of."

"Are you deaf or is it just hard to hear under than helmet?" Maze took a step back. "I said there is no way in hell I'm handing this over to you."

"We'll have to take it then." The Cisk jumped down from their horse and reached for the bag. Instead of getting the bag, they got a fist to the jaw. They stumbled back and looked at him in disbelief.

"Reach for the bag again and you're going to get a lot worse than that." Maze warned the Cisk.

"Nice." Shaw looked at Maze with a smile before addressing the Cisk. Maze shocked him, but he was proud of the way he defended himself. "Well, as you can see, we're not looking to take part in any handoff right now."

"Fine, we'll do this the hard way." The Cisk looked over their head and Shaw followed their line of sight just in time to see the net that dropped over Maze's head. He tried to push Maze out of the way, but was too late.

Shaw looked over his shoulder at Maze just as the net fell over his head.

"What the hell is this?" Maze struggled as he tried to escape into the shadows, but he couldn't. "It's meranium!"

Shaw tried to remove the net but there was no time, the Cisk were quickly surrounding them it wouldn't be long before they were either killed or captured.

"Take the bag and get out of here." Maze told Shaw.

"No, I'm not leaving you here. I'm not losing another partner."

"Shaw, please." Maze urged him to leave, but the peacekeeper had no plans of leaving him there alone.

"Hand over the bag and we'll let you live." The Cisk spoke. "This doesn't have to end in death."

"No," Maze said.

"Not gonna happen." Shaw agreed.

"Fine." The Cisk took a step forward, and a moment later, someone knocked Shaw off his feet.

Instincts took over, and he quickly jumped back to his feet and started fighting, but there were too many. His goal was to keep them away from Maze. No matter how many he knocked out, they kept coming. Shaw drew his daggers to his hands, prepared to do anything, even take a life if it meant keeping Maze protected.

As they closed in on him, tightening the space he had to maneuver, Shaw considered his option. He could shift, bring about a side of him he hadn't in a long time, but he swore he wouldn't do it again. Just as he felt he had no other choice, Shaw looked over and saw a woman running towards him with a weapon in her hand. She took a shot that knocked out two other Cisks.

Taking the advantage of surprise, Shaw pushed harder and fought back the offenders. While he cut them down, the woman ran to Maze and quickly removed the net.

"Who are you?" Shaw asked, happy that she freed Maze, but still concerned about the unexpected presence.

"Think we can do the introduction part later? I'm on your side." She asked, as she flipped the bright red hair out of her face. "For now, that's all you need to know."

"Good enough for me." Maze got to his feet, nodded to both her and Shaw, and stepped into the shadows.

Though Shaw worried about Maze, there wasn't time to voice that concern. Moments later, another two dozen Cisks appeared and joined the fight. The woman impressed Shaw. She skillfully took out the opponent and barely broke a sweat.

"The High Priestess doesn't care about an attack outside her city?" She asked after flipping another attacker on their back.

"Beats me," Shaw said just before punching another Cisk in the jaw. The cracking sound of bone made him smile as he turned on another.

"I guess Mosail isn't the only place with its problems right now." She said as she sized up another Cisk.

"No, it isn't." He grunted and Maze reappeared for a moment, pulling another Cisks into the shadows with him.

The three fought as hard as they could. Even with the Maze using the darkness to their advantage, the Cisks still outnumbered them. Shaw worried they might fail, but then he heard it. The howl of a large gray wolf. The massive wolf caught the Cisks attention, and that alone gave them the advantage they needed.

Moments later, a symphony of growls vibrated the air. Shaw looked around to see eyes glowing in the surrounding trees. They weren't alone. This mystery woman came with some serious backup. Their presence alone was reinforcement enough. The Cisks, made a mad dash for their aerohorses, climbing on their backs and running as fast as they could from the area.

There was one who lingered a moment too long. When they finally tried to flee, the woman dropped to her knee and kicked theirs from beneath them. The Cisk fell to the ground, and with a quick flip, she was on top of them.

"Who are you working for?" She demanded, but they refuse to answer. "Fine, you don't want to cooperate, I'll make this work for myself."

Shaw stepped back when her eyes glowed.

She sat on the Cisk's chest, pinning them to the ground. When they could no longer move, she ripped the protective helmet from their head and forced them to look into her eyes.

"This is going to hurt." She said before digging her thumbs into their eyes.

"Dammit, that's gross." The wolf walked up, body bare in the wind, and Shaw immediately averted his eyes.

"Um." He cleared his throat, then pulled his jacket from his back and handed it to the wolf.

"Oh, thanks." She accepted his offer. When he looked back at her, he recognized her but kept his mouth shut.

While Shaw wondered what such an important wolf was doing in the middle of nowhere helping them fight Cisks, the woman atop their opponent stared out into the distance, clearly no longer seeing them. Maze stepped to his side as she released her target with a deep breath.

"I know who it is." She announced, she stood.

"Who is it?" The wolf asked.

"Someone very powerful." She answered.

"I hate to interrupt, but we need to get moving." Shaw had no idea what they were talking about, but he didn't feel comfortable standing outside of Moon Hollow over more than ten dead Cisks.

"We can't let them get back to Mosail." The mystery woman said, looking down at the person she subdued. "They will tell what happened here."

"I'll handle it." Maze knelt down and placed his hand on the Cisk, and the two vanished.

"K?" She turned to the wolf, confirming further Shaw's

suspicion of who she was. But she didn't say her name. Did the other woman know it?

"Yes." K answered. "What's up, Shan?"

"You up for more adventure or you ready to go home?"

Shaw turned to look at the damage while the two women talked. He didn't need to know the details of their journey, but he was grateful that they'd shown up to help. He caught the tail end of their conversation. K was leaving, Shan was staying.

"You're coming with us?" He asked, making sure he hadn't misheard them.

"Yes, I have to." She answered. "You're going to need me. I don't know why or for what, but you will."

The wolf handed him back his jacket, and Maze reappeared just as she disappeared on the back of an aerohorse.

"Is now a good time for introductions?" He asked.

"Shanoai," the woman said and held her hand out to him.

"I'm Maze." The shadow walker shook her hand. "This is Shaw."

"Nice to meet you both." Shanoai turned to look at the sky when the sound of a dragon's cry rang out in the distance. "I think we have something to take care of."

SHORT:

THE

Librarian

His soft humming traveled the halls of Maistrier. As always, Riza was hard at work perfecting his catalog. One-hundred and seventy-three years he'd worked on his collection. Building from just a few shelves to a massive subterranean stockpile of writings and artifacts. His pride highlighted the history of not only Novia, but the twelve other verses.

It wasn't often he receive visitors. Most gave up when they reached the border wall surround Maistrier, but this was no ordinary day. Days before, he felt the shift in the tide and understood that the energy of their world was changing. It was a sign he knew would come. One he waited for, just as the seer suggested.

Riza, the elf who the ancients chose for his role, counted down the days until the young man would come to collect his prize. Just as told by the first shadow walker to visit his library, on the third day of the third month seventy-five years after the Dragon Queen's slumber, there was a knock on his door. Riza was one to believe in prophecies. When both a seer and a shadow walker speak of the same event, over a decade apart, it's no coincidence.

He jumped down from the tower of books, landing softly on his feet as his mechanical wings retracted. Riza was no ordinary elf. At least not anymore. A decade into his effort, one of the ancients found him and gave him the gift of life everlasting. Now well over two-hundred years old, Riza came up with new ways to navigate the passages of Maistrier.

When he began, it was a simple structure. Most of his collection housed in the shelves above ground. But as time went on and the expansion started, he built down, not out. Beneath the original structure were twenty-three floors surrounding one central shaft he used to move between the floors. The original structure now served as his home. He was too far removed from the general population to ever return to it. Besides, after the elf kingdom fell, dispersing his people, it left nothing for him to return to.

He whistled as he danced down the hall to reach the center shaft. He'd been working on the fourteenth floor, rearranging a collection of miniature dragon statues, when his visitor arrived. When he reached the shaft, those wings expanded and carried him up to the main floor. As he touched down, the hole sealed shut and Riza made his way to the large front door.

Though he used the original structure primarily as his home, it still had plenty of precious items decorating the halls.

Riza straightened himself, pulling his gray hair back into a tight ponytail and placing his hat atop his head. Though he suited up daily, today he wore his very best teal suit with the teardrop collar. It was always a favorite and when he did used to venture outside, he got plenty of compliments on it. He wanted to put his best forward for who he hoped would be a new friend.

With a deep breath to push away his nerves, Riza pulled the massive door open and welcomed his expected visitor.

"Hello." The slender boy spoke nervously. "My name is–"

"I know who you are, Mazeviun Baskiet. And I know why you've come." Riza cleared his throat hoping he didn't sound too eager. "You know, you look just like him. Your grandfather."

"He told you I would come?" The young man with innocent eyes and a nervous expression asked.

"Yes, and to keep a special package for you." He led him through the halls. "Do you know what you've come to retrieve?"

"No. Just that it's important and that I'm supposed to keep it safe. At least, that's what the letter says." The boy held up the crumpled paper. "I wasn't sure if I should come here. I thought this was a joke, but I know it's from him. He's gone now, my grandfather. Died."

"I'm so sorry to hear that. Please come in." Riza stepped aside to let the young man in. "My name is Riza. It's nice to meet you, Mazeviun."

"Maze. You can call me Maze."

"Maze, wonderful."

"It was hard getting here." Maze walked into the home, staring in awe at a large gold statue that sat just left of the door. "Not a lot of shadows, so I had to walk most of the way."

"By design, of course." Riza nodded. "There is a lot here that needs to be protected. Things like what you're here to retrieve. And as you said, it is precious and an important piece of keeping our world safe."

"That important?" Maze stared. "Maybe I should leave it with you. It has to be safer to keep it here."

"Yes, but it can't remain here if it is to serve its purpose." He tapped his finger against the side of Maze's head. "Follow me."

"And you want me to believe that its purpose is with me. I'm just a kid." Maze spoke as he tried to keep up with Riza's long strides. "I don't know what I'm supposed to do with any of this."

"You are young, but you are far from being a child. And regardless, life does not wait for us to feel ready for it to do what it needs." He looked over his shoulder and smiled. "You may be nervous, maybe even afraid, but you're ready to do what needs to be done. Or else you wouldn't be here. Would you?"

229

"Why would he entrust this to me?" Maze asked, and Riza understood he was the only one the young man thought he could speak to about what was happening. "There's so many other people in our family who can do this."

"Yes, there are others, but it is not their destiny. It's yours, whether or not you accept it." Riza adjusted the glasses that sat on the tip of his nose as she stopped walking and turned to the young shadow walker. "Do you accept it?"

Maze nodded.

"Excellent." Riza looked to the left, where three levers stood from the floor. "Pull the second lever and let's get going."

"Me?" Maze pointed at himself, beads of sweat already forming on his brow.

"If you're not strong enough to do this, I have to say I'm worried about how far you'll make it on your journey." Riza pointed to the lever. "Go ahead."

Maze nervously grabbed the lever and looked back at Riza for another confirmation. With some effort, he pulled the lever and when the gears sounded as they engaged. He looked back at Riza with a proud smile. Moments later, the center of the floor opened.

This time, instead of an empty shaft for the librarian to fly down, a platform appeared, and Riza stepped on. With some hesitation, Maze followed.

The librarian tapped the marker on the floor with his foot, and the platform began its descent.

"I can't believe this is happening." Maze shook his head as they moved. Each floor they passed brought more wonders. "How did I get here? You know I only just finished school. I was so excited when we graduated. I really thought it meant I could be free, but now I feel like I'm learning that I'll never be free. Destiny has a plan for me. What I want doesn't matter."

"How did you envision your freedom?" Riza asked as they continued their drop. The eighteenth level was their destination.

"I don't know, maybe getting away from my family's. My mom and current stepdad do nothing but fight. She's afraid he's going to get himself killed, and he's always upset because she keeps getting more debt for him to have to work through. Most of the time, I feel like I'm just adding to the stress.

I've been waiting for the day that I could shadow shift freely so I can get away from them. So I could try to build a life of my own. One that doesn't come with all the stress and drama of being at home. All I had to do was finish school so I could live a legitimate life. But now, if this letter is truly some kind of prophecy, I won't be able to leave home for a very long time."

"May I impart some wisdom on you, young man?" Riza turned to him as the platform stopped moving.

"Seems like if anyone's going to give me wisdom you, you're the one to do it." Maze nodded.

"The first time I met your grandfather, he was a lot like you. He wanted adventure, freedom, and a chance to roam. Not long after that, he stumbled upon a relic. And that discovery changed everything for him. Just like you, he wanted nothing to do with it. Tell me, how much did he put in that letter?" Riza pointed to the crumpled paper that Maze still held in his hand.

"Um..." Maze looked down at it.

"Did he tell you how many times he tried to escape his own destiny? Did he tell you that after he found that relic, he tried to get rid of it? He thought he could find somewhere to just drop it off and keep moving without doing the work required to protect it. Took it as far as The Last Keep trying to get away from the damn thing and you know what happened?"

"What?"

"It found its way back to him. And it kept coming back to him because face wasn't done with him. He had a part to play in all this. Just like you do. And like it or not, the way it works is that you play your part. You can't run from it."

"I can't run."

"No, you can't. And I'll tell you, just like I told your grandfather. Destiny does exactly what it wants, and it doesn't matter what you had planned for yourself. It doesn't care about your desires for your life. But what you can do is work within the path in front of you and find the freedom you want. Even if it doesn't mean that you get to leave home right now."

"You know, I wish I could tell you that makes me feel better, but it doesn't. I still have to go back home and wait. I still have to be miserable while destiny puts the rest of the pieces together."

"Right, well, follow me. No sense and holding things up any longer." Riza stepped off the platform and Maze followed.

They walked down the corridor, passing stacks of books and rooms with locked doors. Riza led the young man to the end of the hall, where a door stood marked with the symbol of the shadow walkers.

232

"This one is for you." He turned to Maze and pulled a small brass key from his pocket to hand over to the young man.

"It's in there?" Maze looked uncomfortably at the door.

"Yes, with all the other things we have about your kind. Not much to my dismay. You shadow walkers don't leave a lot to be found." Riza frowned.

"Sorry about that." Maze shrugged.

"Go ahead." Riza tapped on the door with his knuckle. "Time is ticking."

Maze slid the key into the lock and turned it. The heavy door creaked as the hinges moved for the first time in decades. Inside the room were dust covered shelves that lined the walls and in the center, one table with a box.

Riza stepped inside and lit the candle that sat on the small post next to the entrance.

"I'm assuming this is for me." Maze pointed to the box.

"Your assumption is correct. It's been there, untouched since your grandfather left it here."

"Maybe I should just leave it here. It's good I know where it is now. You know?" Maze turned those innocently hopeful eyes on Riza.

"That would be nice, but its time here has ended. Now its place is with you." Riza nodded.

Maze walked over to the box and touched the surface, wiping the dust from the wood case. The symbol of his people, the shadow walker, etched in the surface. A triangle with a line down the center, and that marker that told him his grandfather touched it.

"This feels overwhelming already. I don't even know what's in the box and yet I feel like it's already changed my life."

"Well, you have an option of finding out now." Riza encouraged him to open the box. He'd never seen its contents either and waited for the day when the boy would come to get it.

Maze lifted the box from the table and cleared the rest of the dust from the surfaces. He examined every angle, then turned to Riza. "How do I open it?"

"You don't know?" Riza frowned. "That is unfortunate."

"No, he didn't exactly give me instructions." Maze looked over the note his grandfather left for him. "It says nothing about how to open this."

"I bet he did, you just have to find them." Riza winked. "Your grandfather was a clever man. I bet you inherited that from him."

"I sure hope so." Maze put the box back on the table. "Now what?"

"Now you take the box, and its mystery contents home with you. You keep it somewhere safe because what's inside there could change the fate of our world. And hopefully, one day, you won't hate your life so much. It just might put you on a path that leads you right that freedom you're looking for."

"What about you? You just gonna stay here in this library with all these books and relics?" Maze looked at Riza. "Don't you want freedom?"

"Inside these walls, I am as free as I could ever be." He smiled. "I've been to so many worlds, experienced so many cultures, through the books and artifacts brought here. I am the keeper of knowledge, the protector of the history of Novia. Do not think that you are the only one with a destiny that crosses with this life." He picked up the box and handed it back to Maze. "Trust me, you're not. I must stay here and protect that which must be found because should you be successful there will always be another threat to come."

"So what's the point? I do this. I succeed. I fulfill my fate and then another threat comes." Maze looked between the box and the man in front of him.

"Exactly. Because this life it doesn't stop, it keeps going, keeps challenging and hopefully the people it chooses will step up to the plate. This time around, life has chosen you for the avenger for the challenge, and as nervous as you are, I know it made the right choice."

"You think so?"

"There's something in you, young shadow walker, something amazing. Though you are afraid, you are brave and that is what the world will need. Take this, keep it somewhere safe and when the time comes, prove yourself worth and life will give you everything you want from it."

If you've enjoyed the journey so far, please take a moment in leave a review!

The collection continues in book 3!

Continue
the journey...

Thank you to our Novian Kickstarter Supporters!

Ace Edmonds
Alana Joli Foster Abbott
Alexis
Alicia McCalla
Alysa Isenhower Hill
Amber Thornton
Angela Williams
Angel-Amanda Brihed
Anna L. Riley
April Hoyes
April Nichole
Ayisha Miles
Barksdale Family
Blaq Intellekt
BriBunny1
Bridgett Evans
Britt
Brittany Miller
Carly Marie Lesoski
Colleen
D Jefferson
David Heyes
Deborah Smallwood
Dee Wiggins
Dia
Drew M
Evangeline Lacey
Florence Delgado
Gabby Angelica Beasley
George Fugh
Gina Da Summoner
Ginger Greaves
Greg Burnham
Hadassah Davids
Heather Tomasello

Holly
I'Asha
Jasmine Hunter
Jasmine Jorden
Jeanine Hurley
Jenee Price
Jess Noel
Joannebj2
Josh
Kashonna Shaw
Keisha Petty
Kelli Fajardo
Kenya
Kevin J. McAdoo
Kimberley Mayfield
Kimyan Gage
Krissi
Kristina Simms
Ladilia keeley
Laneic
LaTasha Oke
Laura
Leah Blue
Linda Sanders
Liza Fraser
Logical Mermaid
Lorraine Counts-Ramirez
Marci Wade
Mary-Beth Roberts
Megan Gruginski
Melodee Chicoine
Mercedes Robinson
Michael Stephens
Michelle Traylor
Mikesha Middlebrook
Mina Snowe
Monique Smith
Msbrunettebooks
nia houston
Nichole Dorsey
Nicole Banks

Nikki
Ninjakat
QuinncySama
Ramona Price
Rhea Alexis M Banks
Ronald S Allen
Rosemary McAleer
Ryan Philbin
Samantha Clark
Sandy Williams
Sarah Gomez
Sean Gilmartin
Shakuita Johnson
Shannon Brent
Shannon Skinner
Sheena
Sid Maria Sineriz
Southern comfort
Stacy Harty
Supersticious Renegade
Tamiya Jones
Tati M
The Creative Fund by BackerKit
Tina Porubsky
Veronica Ard
Wanda Fuller
Whitney Collins
William A Miller III

ABOUT THE AUTHOR

Jessica Cage is an International Award Winning, and USA Today Best-Selling Author. Born and raised in Chicago, IL, writing has always been a passion for her. She dabbles in artistic creations of all sorts, but it's the pen that her hand itches to hold. Jessica had never considered following her dream to be a writer because she was told far too often "There is no money in writing." So she chose the path most often traveled. During pregnancy, she asked herself an important question. How would she be able to inspire her unborn son to follow his dreams and reach for the stars, if she never had the guts to do it herself? Jessica took a risk and unleash the plethora of characters and their crazy adventurous worlds that had previously existed only in her mind into the realm of readers. She did this with hopes to inspire not only her son but herself. Inviting the world to tag along on her journey to become the writer she has always wanted to be. She hopes to continue writing and bringing her signature Caged Fantasies to readers everywhere.

Find out more about Jessica on her website: www.jessicacage.com

CPSIA information can be obtained
at www.ICGtesting.com
Printed in the USA
LVHW092007160223
739678LV00004B/548